Every fiber in her being screamed in protest when he withdrew his arm.

Her soul cried out for him to instead take her into a full embrace. To kiss her again not just on the cheek but on her lips, her neck and even more intimate spots on her body.

That was never to be. She was going to parade around Cannes with a dynamic and noble prince. But that would be that.

Not only would there be no romance with Zander, there couldn't even be hot reckless nights where she'd satisfy her attraction to him and then be done with it. The prince's casual-affair days were over. Which was just as well because, if she was being honest, Marie didn't think she could handle a fling with him that would come to an abrupt end.

Although she knew that she'd spend the rest of her life remembering his one and only kiss on the cheek and his strong arm around her.

But Marie and Zander were in a business relationship. One she was fortunate to have.

Any other thoughts were just pure self-torture.

Dear Reader,

It must have been the wedding of Prince Harry and Meghan Markle, which was taking place while I was writing this book. But this American girl hadn't given much thought to the role of young royals in a long time, to their unique opportunity to effect good in the world. My book's hero, Prince Zander, considers it both his privilege and his duty to devote himself to worthy causes (one of them being a little soft-cheeked bundle less than two feet tall). Don't we all love a powerful hero with a heart of gold?

Marie has had it rough. And the last thing she expects is to develop feelings for a sophisticated, unattainable prince! Between her barriers and his, a future together is highly unlikely. Funny how love has the ability to smash walls to the ground.

So let's go to the French Riviera and peek in on their story. Expect glamorous parties, gorgeous clothes and the finest bubbly. It can be our little secret that we're in pajamas, curled up in our favorite chair and sipping tea.

Andrea x

The Prince's Cinderella

Andrea Bolter

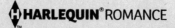

Recycling programs
for this product may
not exist in your area.

ISBN-13: 978-1-335-49929-5

The Prince's Cinderella

First North American publication 2019

HARLEQUIN®
www.Harlequin.com

Printed in U.S.A.

Andrea Bolter has always been fascinated by matters of the heart. In fact, she's the one her girlfriends turn to for advice with their love lives. A city mouse, she lives in Los Angeles with her husband and daughter. She loves travel, rock 'n' roll, sitting at cafés and watching romantic comedies she's already seen a hundred times. Say hi at andreabolter.com.

Books by Andrea Bolter

Harlequin Romance

Her New York Billionaire
Her Las Vegas Wedding
The Italian's Runaway Princess

Visit the Author Profile page at Harlequin.com.

For Lauren

Praise for
Andrea Bolter

"This is Ms. Bolter's debut novel though it doesn't show.... The characters are well rounded and have a touch of reality that allows them to flow off of the page and into our imagination."

—*Harlequin Junkie* on *Her New York Billionaire*

CHAPTER ONE

"WELCOME TO THE headquarters of the APCF," Felice Khalif said to Marie as they proceeded down a row of work cubicles. There was a hum in the air, with the people at every desk either on the phone or focused on the computer screens in front of them. At the back of the space, Felice pointed to a small office separated from the central area by a glass wall and door. "Here's where you'll be working."

The partitioned-off room wasn't large but Marie had never had a private office before so she had to admit it gave her a buzz. Inside, a sleek glass desk was topped with boxes and stacks of paper files. A telephone bank was off to one side. Four chrome chairs sat around a glass meeting table. One large canvas with an abstract design painted in pastel colors adorned the wall.

The lone window didn't look out to the glitzy beachfront Promenade de la Croisette that Cannes on the French Riviera was known for but it did let in plenty of light. Not that it mattered, though. Marie was here to work, not to daydream out the window.

"When our events manager, Jic Gurov, suddenly quit, Alain at the Toulouse office recommended I bring you in," Felice continued. "We'll give it a try temporarily. You'll have to jump right in. We have so much going on, and I don't really have anyone to train you."

"I'll do my best." Marie brushed her bangs away from her eyes. This was a career opportunity she could have never seen coming. A million thanks were due to Alain for recommending her for the job. Not only did he understand about the work in Toulouse that she'd had to leave unfinished, he'd also given her a glowing recommendation.

"I prepared this much for you." Felice handed Marie a single piece of paper. "Here are the upcoming events that I can confirm."

"Thanks."

Felice was right that everything was happening so fast. One minute Marie was assistant to the events coordinator for the APCF, Alliance for Parentless Children of France, at its regional office in Toulouse, and now she was at the headquarters in Cannes with a chance to become the permanent events manager if she did a good job.

France's largest nonprofit agency supporting orphaned children was a well-known organization with several field offices throughout the country. The agency was able to aid parentless children who were in the foster care system with case management, social services and transitional assistance into adulthood. An orphan herself, Marie had utilized the agency's help when she was a teenager, and the organization hired her for a job after university.

"As you know, the most important date on the calendar is our annual fund-raising gala in three weeks. The proceeds from that evening finance all of our operations for the year."

"Alain told me."

"Unfortunately, I don't think Jic has compiled all of the components for this event. Zander is coming by today to go over it with you in detail."

"Who's Zander?"

Felice heard her phone's ping and answered it. "Yes? I'll call her right back."

Marie imagined that as the agency's executive director, Felice must have many balls to juggle in the air at once. She had a matter-of-fact manner that was very professional. In her cream-colored suit, Felice lifted her eyeglasses from the chain hanging around her neck and put them on to respond to something else on her phone.

After smoothing the front of her gray trousers to try to straighten out any creases, Marie stood as tall as she could. She subtly reached behind her to tuck her blouse in tighter. At the office in Toulouse she did occasionally meet with important donors and was included in meetings, so she never dressed too informally for work. But if Felice's high-end suit was any indication, Marie might need to up her look here. After all, this was Cannes, land of the rich and famous.

At this point, she certainly didn't have money to go out and buy a new wardrobe, as much fun as that sounded. Taking a mental inventory of the clothes she did have, she figured she could put together a week of decent outfits to get started.

If she let it, Marie's mind could start swirling. There hadn't been any chance for the logistics of this unexpected job switch to be worked out. The agency was able to provide a room for her to stay in for the time being in one of its housing facilities in Cannes. But if the job became permanent, she'd have to find an apartment and give up the room she leased in Toulouse. Cannes would be a much more expensive place to live so she didn't know what she'd be able to afford. Then again, if she were to get this position permanently, there'd be a substantial salary increase.

She'd have to keep the uncertainty from getting to her during this trial period. Temporary things didn't always work out for her. One thing Marie Paquet had known all of her life was impermanence. There might be more of it to accept. Would that ever stop, would there ever be something in her life that she could count on?

Taking in the slow, measured breaths that her years spent in counseling taught her, she centered herself.

A young man came into the office and handed Felice a laptop. "Thank you, Clive."

Marie followed Felice's lead in bringing their chairs close together so that they could sit down at the table and huddle in front of the laptop. "This will be for your use. The login you had in Toulouse will work for general access. I'll give you another password to get into the files we keep confidential because they contain donor information."

"Do you know if the system logs the events chronologically, or alphabetically, or in some other order?"

"Let's hope it's chronologically so that you can prioritize." Felice opened the laptop and clicked through several folders until she found what she was looking for. "Voila."

"Great." Marie was relieved that the files were located. She was going to need all the help she could get.

"Look at your list and tell me if this corresponds. Of course, the gala in May. The Regional Managers Retreat Weekend in June?"

Marie reviewed her list. "Yes. The entry says five meals. Two dinners, two breakfasts and one lunch. Continuous snack and beverage service for both days. Transportation to and from the hotel. Multiple media setups. Breakout classrooms. Writing supplies. Goody bags. Then there's a handwritten note in red to check the hotel."

Felice opened another folder. "Donor Appreciation Luncheon in July?"

"Yes, I have that on the list although there are no specifics except winery picnic."

"Goodness, there's almost nothing in here," Felice sighed as she opened that file. "You'll have to look though this yourself and see if there's anything useful. It looks like Jic recorded his notes from meetings but didn't highlight any decisions."

Marie grabbed a pen and jotted Felice's instructions onto her printed list.

"Next, Back-to-School Support Suppers in September."

Marie's fists opened and closed repeatedly. How well she remembered those suppers that the agency hosted to aid kids in foster care who were beginning their new school years. For some, including Marie, the start of the school year was wrought with either dread or apprehension. Dread if the previous year hadn't gone well but they were returning to the same school. And apprehension if they were starting at a new school.

Kids could be cruel. But to orphans and other children in foster care, mercilessly so. The unkind ones already knew who the foster kids were, and would find ways to taunt and tease them. They'd yell out meanness to Marie that she was unwanted. That she had no family. That nobody loved her. Like many in her situation, Marie grew a thick outer shell and learned not to cry in front of the bullies. Not that she didn't shed a million tears in private.

The September suppers the agency held had been a godsend for Marie. Psychologists, social workers and education specialists were all on hand to discuss problems and develop strategies. Without them, the pressure of the new school year might have swallowed Marie up and left her too isolated and anxious to have succeeded in her classes.

Now she was going to be part of creating those dinners that had meant so much to her. As an adult, she had long accepted the fact that she would never be part of a typical family. But by working at the agency she was in some small way making other orphans feel that somebody cared about them. In that, she felt great pride and satisfaction.

"There's a note on my list to check the budget after the gala," Marie reported to Felice.

"We'll have to see what funding the gala brings in, in order to determine how much money we can spend on the September suppers and how many of them we can offer throughout the country."

"Of course."

As a teen, it had never occurred to Marie how programs the APCF provided were financed. Only that they were able to help with the extra services people might not be able to afford. Orphaned children sometimes had mental health issues such as depression or post-traumatic stress disorder. Others had learning disabilities or physical conditions. And, maybe most important, once they reached adulthood there was often no place for them to turn for transitional help into higher education or the workforce. The APCF did as much as it could for as many as it could.

Once she started working for the organization, Marie understood that any money it spent on its programs came from outside donations. She glanced up from her powwow with Felice and thanked the air surrounding her that this agency existed and that she was brought into it by one of her few schoolteachers who cared. A quick wince reminded her of some who didn't.

"I need to return a call." Felice looked up from her phone to Marie. "Why don't you continue to match up your notes and see how much information you have?"

"Okay."

"Zander has all of the data for the gala on his own computer. He's very specific about what he wants. He'll go over that with you. We're lucky to have him chairing the event this year, so let's make every effort to facilitate his plans."

"Who's Zander?" Marie realized that Felice hadn't answered when she'd asked the first time.

"Felice!" a shrill voice called out from the main office space.

"Let me go deal with that—" Felice stood up "—and let's touch base at the end of the day. After Zander comes."

As the director charged out the door, Marie asked yet again, this time to the back of her jacket, "*Who* is Zander?"

What a difference a year made.

Zander de Nellay surveyed the sweeping view of the Cannes shoreline through the floor-to-ceiling sliding glass doors of his posh penthouse. The palm-tree-lined promenade of La Croisette followed the crescent-shaped curve of the sparkling Gulf of Napoule and its white-sand beaches. It was a sight to behold, indeed.

Little, if nothing, of the vista appeared any different from how it had last spring. Although then, as he had in years past, Zander had stayed in an elegant suite at one of the grand dame hotels on the promenade. And had partied every night with Hollywood film producers and the *glamorati* who flocked to Cannes from all over the world.

This season, he'd instead be ensconced in a penthouse apartment that kept the town's constant revelry at arm's length.

Gliding one of the doors open, he stepped out onto the terrace. The sun was bright but the air was crisp, a combination he'd always enjoyed. Cannes in late spring was a marvelous place to be.

Fortunately, to Zander's precise specifications, the rental agent was able to find him a suitable penthouse with a terrace that was walled-in cement rather than the typical iron balcony railing, which he wouldn't have trusted was safe enough for eighteen-month-old Abella, even though he knew she would never be outside on her own. But securely enclosed, Zander could create a little play area out here for her so that she could get plenty of the fresh sea air. He'd just need a patio umbrella or other covering to shelter her from the strength of the sun.

He shook his head to himself. A year ago Zander was an unattached bachelor, much to his mother's chagrin, with thoughts only of what suited him. He rotated his life between time spent in his native Charlegin, his apartment in Paris's tony Sixth Arrondissement and his travels throughout the world on behalf of his charitable endeavors.

Now his mind was on baby-safe balconies.

Stepping back into the penthouse's sitting room, he watched the deliveries arriving.

Movers carried in the petal-pink upholstered rocking chair he'd had sent from his apartment in Paris. Rather than buying one here in Cannes, he wanted the exact chair that Abella had become comfortable with. Truth be told, he was accustomed to it, too. He loved quietly sitting in that chair with her.

Yes, one of the most eligible playboys in Europe now found himself preferring to rock baby Abella in his arms than cavorting with the high society he'd always been surrounded by. And Zander was keenly aware of the realness exchanged between them in those moments.

Heading toward the master bedroom suite, he saw Iris, a compact woman in her sixties who had been Abella's nanny since the day she was born. "Is she asleep?"

"She's just starting to rouse."

There went that funny tap in the center of Zander's chest. It was a sensation that had arrived around a year ago. The mere thought of seeing Abella pulled at his heart. Her cherubic pink cheeks and that cute way she stretched her back after a nap as if she'd been farming in the fields all day.

"The wardrobe is here," one of his assistants announced as Zander entered the master suite. "I believe you wanted to go over it."

Zander didn't really envision himself as fussy when it came to clothes. But with all the charitable organizations he endorsed and all of the fund-raising benefits and balls he attended, his wardrobe had to be appropriate. He'd come to Cannes for the spring social season and would be attending a dozen formal events and countless others that called for business attire. Even the black slacks and black shirt he wore at the moment were bespoke from the finest tailor in London.

"Create a file for me of what I'm wearing from head to toe for each event so that I don't have to think about it on that given day," he instructed the assistant. With Abella's care always on his mind, it was more important than ever that he simplify everything else. Plus, while in Cannes he planned to devote himself to chairing the APCF gala and making it the event of the season, and he needed as much time as possible to do so.

In fact, he'd be leaving the penthouse soon to go to the APCF office to meet with the event manager there. The agency's director, Felice, had informed him that the previous manager had suddenly left. Zander hoped his replacement would be up to the task of creating the kind of spectacular evening he had in mind.

If there was one thing Zander knew about, it was raising money. He made a great deal of public appearances to support good works all over the world. He gave his time and his notability freely, making it his life's work in fact. Now it was payback time. He expected many of his wealthy friends and acquaintances to donate generously to the APCF gala.

"I'll wear the white-jacketed tux for the Clean Water for Africa fund-raiser," he began. Most of the tuxedos were all black. One had traditional notch lapels, another a thin shawl collar that gave it a retro look. "This one for the cocktail reception with the film festival judges."

Another was made of velvet, a fabric that was considered very chic right now although Zander wasn't convinced it suited him. He didn't assign that one to an evening. There was the two-button he'd wear with a black shirt. Then the charcoal with the double-breasted jacket, the navy with the black lapels that he quite liked, the all-navy one and the peak-lapel gunmetal gray.

"White shirt with everything but the two-button."

Finally, he inspected the unusual tuxedo for the Mexican-themed gala that his stylist had ordered. With heavy black embroidery atop the shinier black fabric of the jacket's lapels, it was a unique piece that would fit well with the evening.

After rattling off instructions for everything from cuff links to socks, Zander turned to the second closet. There were a dozen suits with coordinating shirts, ties and shoes. Casual clothes suitable for boating or country drives. Golf and tennis wear. Beach attire. Everything was in order.

Except his mind. Thoughts of the constant socializing and the superficial women who gravitated toward him, who cared only about what they could get from him, all felt so stale. Maybe it was the baby, but a longing was starting to grow in him. For something different. Something new.

He'd RSVP'd for all the season's events as a party of two, not willing to face the firing squad alone, but really having no idea whom he'd bring along as his plus one. He'd planned to think of a platonic friend he could make easy chitchat with. Who wouldn't immediately misread his invitation to accompany him as a proposal into his world.

Misjudging a woman's intentions had only too recently stung him hard.

Frankly, he couldn't think of a woman who would fit the bill, but he'd deal with that later.

Zander left his bedroom suite. Although he told himself he'd only poke his head in to see if she was fully awake, he instead gently pushed open the door and slipped into baby Abella's bedroom.

"Well, look at you, Bell-bell." She was sitting upright in her crib, her curly blond hair tousled this way and that. "You're all the way awake already."

"Up time," she said, having only recently begun attempts at true conversation. "Up."

"Yes, Bell-bell. Up."

No further prompting was required. Zander hurried to the side of her crib to reach in, put each of his hands under the baby's arms and lift her out. He brought her against his left shoulder, as had become his routine after Iris had taught him the proper way to securely hold a baby. Zander could never figure out what the *gaga* noise Abella made was meant to signify, but she always did it when he picked her up.

She twisted herself sideways a bit to stare at Zander's face.

His eyes met hers. It was like looking in a mirror. Those dark brown, almost black, almond-shaped eyes that they had in common. The same almond eyes that his sister, Elise, had had. He could never look at Abella without thinking of his sister, his heart shattering at missing her so. Wishing he could rewrite the past so that Elise could be here right now and see how much Abella was growing and developing.

Zander and Abella continued the eye lock that they did frequently. Which he took as some kind of unspoken declaration of mutual love.

"Da," Abella said.

Da. As in Daddy.

"No, Bell-bell. Uncle Zander. Can you say Zander?"

"Da."

"Zan. How about you say Zan?"

"Da."

Each time she uttered that syllable it was with more determination and certainty than the time before, despite his protests. The word filled Zander with confusion about the decisions that were going to have to be made. Maybe not today, but soon.

He held the baby closer, inhaling the lovely smell of that fruity, organic and toxin-free shampoo Iris used on her hair.

As Zander carried Abella into the living room, a grocer arrived with food. Iris came toward him to take Abella if that was what he so desired.

Not ready to let go just yet he said, "I'll hold her for a while."

With all the comings and goings, the front door was left open. Three quick knocks against the doorjamb brought Zander's attention. It was the penthouse's rental agent, who upon spotting Zander, folded one arm rigidly across his waist and bowed forward. He sputtered in a nervous voice, "Is everything to your liking, Your Highness?"

Four hours passed before Marie looked up from her laptop. Having combed through every single file her predecessor, Jic, had left, she finally had a grasp of what information there was and what more was required for her to move forward with the APCF events calendar.

She hadn't been privy to why Jic abruptly up and left his position, only that he'd had some personal problems to attend to. The fact that some of the files were in decent shape and others were an indecipherable hodge-podge told her that Jic's departure had been hasty and unplanned. He hadn't left clear instructions for whoever was to take over. Marie had made as many notes as she could and jotted down questions to ask Felice at the end of the day.

Out of the corner of her eye, she noticed something dark beyond the glass separating her office from the main work floor. As she lifted her face from the computer screen, what met her gaze was quite a surprise.

A man had his arm up, hand making a fist as if he was just about to knock on the glass to get her attention. But it wasn't just any man. It was, without question, the most attractive man Marie had ever seen in her life. At least six feet three inches tall, he wore a black shirt tucked into black pants with a brown belt, topped by a brown jacket. She thought the combination of the black and brown was impossibly tasteful.

The color palette didn't stop with the clothes. His unusually shaped eyes were the darkest of browns, practically black, with his defined bone structure forming an unforgettable face. The crowning touch was a full head of thick, straight blond hair, expertly cut so that some fell forward from his forehead and the rest stayed put around his ears. Marie was sure there was never a hair out of place on the man's head.

Because he had frozen midknock, it was as if she was looking at a still photo. So she jolted when he moved to lower his arm and flash her a megawatt smile. His perfectly white teeth all but glistened in the office's harsh overhead lighting. Marie smiled back, no idea who he was or why he was in her doorway. But it wasn't often—okay, never—that an elegant and gorgeous man was grinning at her. She'd be crazy not to smile back.

While it was difficult to do anything but sit there and stare at the magnificent specimen of the human race, it occurred to Marie that she should get up and open the door to see who he was. Standing and moving toward him, she hoped her pants weren't too creased from sitting at the computer for so long. She hadn't checked her hair in hours, either, and knew that it could be an absolute mop at this point. Her lipstick had faded ages ago.

There was nothing she could do about any of that.

"Can I help you?" Marie asked after opening her door.

"Are you Marie?"

"Yes."

"Felice suggested I see you."

"Okay."

"I'm Zander de Nellay."

Oh. The gala's chairperson. Marie had been reading about him in the files.

Jic had noted three facts about Zander. Wants what he wants. Insists everything be

of top-notch quality. Offering to pay the difference if anything goes over budget.

That seemed fair enough to Marie. On the
private handwritten notes, Jic had doodled
a little crown above Zander's name. Marie
wondered if Jic was indicating that he was
kind of a diva, or thought he was a king, or
that he was formal and fussy.

"Marie Paquet." She thrust out her hand
for a handshake. His joined hers in what she
figured would be a traditional business greet-
ing between two people who had never met.

The last thing she was expecting was for
his hand to be big and strong and to convey
friendliness rather than protocol. She surely
wasn't prepared for the affection coming from
the center of his palm to slide up her arm and
down the entire right side of her body, so ro-
bust it actually made her torso bend toward it.

Once she was able to stand up straight
again, she gestured for him to enter her office and closed the door behind them.

"I'm sorry. I've just started today so I
haven't had a chance to set up," Marie felt
compelled to explain. She didn't want him
thinking she was some kind of slob with the
boxes and stacks of paper everywhere clut-
tering up such a nice office. That was a sore
spot with her because once people learned

about her troubled upbringing, they assumed she was somehow unorganized or nonfunctional. It was always an uphill battle to prove them wrong.

"That's fine," Zander dismissed her concern. "This was Jic's office up until a couple of days ago and it was in the same condition then."

"Do you know why he left so suddenly?"

"I was expecting you to have the answer to that question."

"I'm sorry I don't."

Marie brushed her bangs to the side and tamped down her hair. She didn't know why she was nervous around this man, other than that he was the gala chair. It wasn't just that he was good-looking. Maybe it was that he had an undeniable air of style and class about him. Which was something Marie always admired in people. Traits that she surely knew nothing about, having grown up in whatever was the opposite of *grace* and *refinement*.

Wow, Zander de Nellay was tall. Fairly petite herself, Marie had to lean her head back to see his eyes. Although she didn't like his expression when he looked down at her. Because she imagined he was looking *down at her*.

And she'd sure as heck had enough of that in her life.

Marie reminded herself that she was projecting that onto Zander. She didn't know him well enough to be able to read his thoughts on anything, and he didn't know anything about her. A man like him, chair of a huge charity event, wearer of fine clothes, possessor of a splendid face, probably wasn't even thinking about how inexpensive Marie's trousers were or that she needed a haircut.

"Can I offer you a water or a coffee?" Felice had stressed that she was to do everything she could to assist Zander.

"I brought some." He placed his computer bag onto one of the chairs around the meeting table and pulled out his laptop and a bottle of gourmet sparkling water. "Do you have cups?"

Marie looked around the office she'd not yet had a minute to personalize. Near the telephone was a stack of disposable cups. "It seems I do," she reported and reached for them.

Zander twisted the cap off the bottle with a flourish Marie couldn't help but note. When a bit of carbonation from inside was set free, it hissed. Which was exactly how Marie was starting to feel in Zander's presence. Like she might need to let out some bubbles soon so as not to explode.

After the drinks were poured and Zander had booted up his laptop, they began.

"Why don't you bring your chair closer and we can work from my screen?" he suggested.

Even though she'd been in the exact same configuration with Felice earlier in the day, sitting next to Zander was another proposition entirely. Her awareness of him was palpable. His entire body emanated warmth. It hadn't been coming from just his palm when he'd shaken her hand.

Her fists opened and closed involuntarily.

Zander reached in his bag for something else. But when he glanced at what he retrieved, a quick smirk flashed across his face and he stuffed whatever it was back in. A second dig yielded the USB drive he'd been searching for. Naturally, curiosity racked Marie as to what the first item was.

"As I understand it," he said while reading, "the components are venue, theme, invitations, arrivals. Then there is food and beverages, rentals of tables and chairs, tableware, bar setup, buffets. Flowers, linens, tech, photography, band, auction, speeches and volunteers."

"The venue is booked and invitations have been sent, according to Jic's notes."

"Yes, months ago. Have you seen them?"

"No, I've only just started on the job today."

"There's no need to make excuses. I was merely asking if you'd seen them."

"I'm sorry. I hope they're in one of these boxes." Marie pointed to the disarray she'd inherited on her desk.

"And no need to apologize." Zander reached into his bag again and located one of the invitations. He handed it to Marie.

Wants what he wants. Marie reread Jic's note about Zander. That was fine. Marie was detail oriented, too. That's how she'd gotten as far as she had in the APCF agency. By learning to be diligent. Not a skill she'd had any example of growing up. Except maybe toward all the wrong things.

The lavender cardstock invitation had all of the basic information. The name of the mansion that had been converted into a party location. The event date and time.

"I thought of these as more of a *save the date* kind of announcement," Zander commented. "They have no pizzazz. And they don't mention the theme."

"Had a theme been decided on? I don't see anything about it in my notes."

"No. And with three weeks to go, it's rather late in the game to be planning a big theme. But we must. I want this to be one of the most successful benefits of the social season. We have to pull out all of the stops."

Marie only theoretically understood what Zander was saying. She'd heard of lavish balls in which moneyed guests came dressed as animals or as gangsters from the 1920s. High concepts that were designed to make the evening as impressive as it could be. With the idea that would bring in the highest donations, sponsorships and auction proceeds.

"I've only been associated with this organization for a year myself," Zander said as he scrolled through his files. "Has the annual APCF gala utilized a theme in the past? How big were the previous galas?"

"I don't know. I'll get back to you as soon as I can with that information."

"I understand that the APCF's invitation list is five hundred. And I've added my own personal five hundred. Has the agency hosted a fund-raiser of that size before?"

"I'll get the answer to that as soon as I can."

"How do you not know this? Didn't they brief you?"

"I'm sorry," Marie started again, but was getting pretty tired of apologizing. "As soon as I gather all of the information, I'll report back to you." Felice hadn't had time to fill her in on the history of the galas and Zander being so on top of everything was very intimidating.

No matter how big an event this was going to be, Marie knew she could get the job done once she had a grasp on it. It was crucial that she show Felice and the other agency bigwigs that she was capable of this position. It was time for her to take a next step up in her career, and this was an unexpected opportunity for her to show what she could do.

Proving naysayers wrong was something she'd spent a lot of her life doing. Frustration crinkled her face when she wondered if she'd ever be finished selling herself to others. Who usually doubted her from the start.

"All right." Zander made some sort of internal decision and proclamation. He transmitted full authority in every word he said, every gesture he made. Whoever he was other than chairperson for this gala, he was a force to be reckoned with. That's the kind of person Marie wanted to be. Maybe she could learn something from him. "We need to get you up to speed, and immediately."

"Yes."

Zander tapped a number into his phone. "Iris, are you able to manage until this evening?"

Whoever Iris was and whatever she was

telling him made him grin. And my, a smiling Zander de Nellay was a sight to behold. No wonder his chairing this gala was such a big deal. That smile could coax a wallet right out of its pocket.

Finishing the call, he returned his attention to Marie. "I'm starved. Let's go get some food. We'll work through the files and see where we are on every component," he commanded as if his will was always obeyed. One thing was for sure. Zander was the most compelling man Marie had ever met.

CHAPTER TWO

HALF OF ZANDER'S mind was on Marie Paquet, the young woman beside him as they left the APCF office and walked toward the center of town. The rest of his brain was on Abella, the not yet two-foot-tall girl who was the most important person in the world to him. When he'd called home, Iris let him know that everything was under control at the penthouse so that he didn't have to worry about rushing back.

That was a relief, what with the moving people and deliveries coming through, and Abella's needs to be considered. He made a mental note to give Iris some extra days off with pay once they were all settled in. A funny little trio, he, the baby niece and the widowed nanny. But a working unit nonetheless.

To the matter of the gala, he'd yet to conclude whether Marie was going to be a help or a hindrance. She seemed oddly unaware of his royal status so he'd made a point of not telling her. Because as soon as people found out, they acted differently around him. Either nervous to the point of flubbing up simple tasks, or going into overdrive to be perfect. Most people were flustered in the company of His Highness Prince Zander de Nellay of Charlegin.

It was surprising that she didn't know who he was, but it seemed there were a lot of gaps in what she'd been informed of. So at least in this first encounter, he'd let her think of him only as the event chair whom she had to satisfy, without the added distraction and onus of his title. Perhaps they'd get to know each other a bit first.

He'd come off brusque when they'd met in the office. No one could blame him, though, for being frustrated that, while he was responsible for this crucial fund-raising gala, the agency had undergone a personnel change and Marie, the replacement, was unapprised on more than just his identity.

"Do you know a place?" she asked, reshuffling the weight of a tote bag filled with paperwork on one shoulder and her laptop under the other arm.

"This way."

Reaching over to take Marie's bag off her

shoulder, an unexpected sensation greeted him. As his fingertips grazed the thin fabric of her blouse in the process, Zander stiffened a little bit. His body suddenly piqued with alertness. For a good twenty paces after that, he was unable to divert his thoughts from wondering what the skin under that white shirt of Marie's might feel like if he slipped his hand underneath it. Soft as satin, he was sure of it.

It was a strange fascination. He hadn't felt curiosity about a woman in a long time.

"Do you live in Cannes?" Marie brought him back to the moment with her question, looking up to him with her big and almost completely round light blue eyes.

"I come down for the social season every spring."

"Down from where?"

"I keep an apartment in Paris. And my home is in Charlegin."

"Where is that?"

"It's a small principality near the Belgium border."

"What do you do there?"

Mashing his lips together, he suppressed a response. He wasn't used to being asked such direct inquiries. Once people knew who he was, they usually became tongue-tied or fluffed on about the weather or the rosebushes. Marie's candor was intriguing, if unknowingly inappropriate.

"I'm involved in several charitable organizations," he answered in absolute truth. "May I?" He gestured at her laptop, taking it and slipping it into his bag alongside his own computer.

Tucking it in, his fingers again made contact with the incongruous item he had encountered when looking for the USB drive while he and Marie were still at the office. Inadvertently squeezing the malleable plastic, a quack sound echoed through the leather. How one of Abella's bath toys, the squidgy yellow duck, ended up in his bag he'd never know.

"What was that?" Marie asked in response to the sound.

"Oh, nothing." He wasn't ready to explain just yet, having learned the hard way that women tended to *ooh* and *aah* when they found out that the eligible prince was caring for a baby. And then tried to convince him that by decree of their gender they could do a better job of it than he was. When, in his experience, they were only trying to take care of themselves by worming their way into his world.

A hurtful pang reminded him that only a few months ago he'd been duped into just that.

Nothing about Marie suggested she was of that breed. But he wasn't going to be deceived, or put Abella's safety in jeopardy, ever again.

He led them to a pedestrians-only block where every other business was a café. Outdoor tables extended as far as the eye could see, each shaded from the sun with cloth awnings or umbrellas in a riot of colors. People sat chatting in groups, nursing aperitifs. Romantic couples leaned in close as they shared pastries.

Picking one of the cafés he thought he remembered from his time here last year, Zander instructed the hostess to seat them at one of the outside tables. With a pull on Marie's chair, he helped her sit and then took the wicker chair opposite her.

"Café au lait?" he suggested and after her confirmation, he ordered when the waiter arrived.

Quickly perusing the menu, he chose an herbed omelet. Marie took a bit longer to decide but once the waiter returned with the coffees, they had both made their selections.

"This is so scenic," Marie said as she surveyed the panorama from the café's patio. Palm trees dotted the horizon beyond the low buildings that lined the block. The air was clean and the sky was blue.

"Yes, Cannes is a very special place. Where are you from?"

She hesitated before answering. "North Marseilles, originally. But I was working for the APCF in Toulouse before this."

"And you've been called to service in Cannes."

"It's a great opportunity for me."

"You have no children? Parents? No husband or boyfriend to consider in a relocation?"

Marie looked downward before lifting her head only slightly and answering through her eyelashes. "No. It's just me."

Zander felt a bloom in his gut at finding out that Marie was unattached. Which was ridiculous, as if his body was betraying him. What matter was it of his whether Marie was married or spoken for?

Perhaps he was just curious. Just a year ago he was the playboy bachelor entrenched in the social scene of young royals. Where he spent his days, and nights, in the company of stunning women.

Until the world as Prince Zander knew it

came crashing down. When his sister, Princess Elise, and her husband, Prince Valentin, were killed in a plane crash. And Abella, at the time six months old, was put in Zander's care.

The peculiar thing was, shifting from the jet-setter who dated the most desirable women in the most exotic places and enjoyed enviable pursuits of leisure was a much easier change than anyone would have guessed.

Truthfully, Zander had become tired of romping around. He was especially worn down by the people he met who were interested only in his title and his standing. Who never saw him for who he really was, what he cared about inside. As was personified by the one mistaken go-round with the woman who confirmed all of his suspicions.

After that, it was crystal clear. Tragedy was the catalyst for short-circuiting Prince Zander's lifestyle. But it was as easy as flipping a switch for him to turn his attention to one female and one female only. One who was hopefully eating her diced peaches before readying herself for a sleep.

His sister, Elise, was two years older than him, the firstborn. Which meant that Abella, her only child, was the crown princess and heir to the throne. Zander was responsible for raising not only a child, but the future ruler of their native Charlegin.

It all added up to why Zander had toy duckies in his briefcase and diced peaches on his mind. He could have hardly been bestowed a more important task than caring for Abella. Which provided a reason for him to stop surrounding himself with untrustworthy people whom he didn't even really know. He had to be very cautious with whom he brought into his orbit now, as he had the baby princess to protect.

Which was why, Zander reflected as the waiter delivered the food, the personal life of this lovely Mademoiselle Marie across the table from him should be of no interest of his.

So why was it?

Zander thought he'd seen a wash of sadness come across Marie's face when he asked if there were people in her life she was concerned about leaving behind in Toulouse.

With those big blue pools for eyes and a rose-petal mouth, she was a natural beauty. Her brown hair was a bit of a fright, with too-long fringy bangs and unruly waves tossing her locks this way and that. Yet her porcelain skin, which was so pale it was translucent, captivated his attention.

After they'd had a few bites of food for

sustenance, Zander was ready to get down to business.

"In my opinion the most unforgettable galas start with a big thematic concept. It adds magic and theatricality."

"We had a hot-air balloon theme for a fund-raiser I worked on," Marie offered. "We carried it through all of the details. Table centerpieces that were small versions of the balloons with flowers coming out of the baskets. And we had party favors with miniature balloons filled with chocolates."

Zander chose his words carefully. "Marie, I'd consider that more a decorating scheme than an event theme."

Her eyes got wide. He knew she'd felt criticized, which was not his intention. But if he was going to chair a gala that was to be on par with the lavish affairs the social season was known for, Marie was going to have to expand her thinking. "I'm talking about the no-holds-barred extravaganzas like, for example, the Carnival balls that Venice is known for. They are drenched in theme from top to bottom, with venues and costumes and dinners that take your breath away."

"The APCF doesn't typically do galas on that scale."

"That's why they asked me to chair. They

need to raise the kind of money the larger organizations do. So we've decided that throwing the most memorable benefit of the season will be the kickoff to a new level of fundraising."

"I'll do my best. I've worked on dozens of events."

In reality, Zander had very clear ideas of what he wanted to do. He didn't need a sort of event manager who might not consult with him about every facet of the party. If his name was going to be linked with the APCF, everything was going to be *his* way. Perhaps someone with less experience like Marie would be a plus. He was willing to spend the next couple of days finding out if they worked well together.

With a charming smile she asked, "Do you have a personal connection to parentless children?"

That reminded him that she still didn't know who he was.

Which, actually, struck him as more than a little strange. Had she never seen his name in the news?

Sadly, Elise's and Valentin's deaths, and Zander's role in raising Abella, had garnered a lot of coverage. The story was picked up by all of the outlets when the plane crash happened a year ago. Bachelor Prince Now Daddy Day Care and plenty of other embarrassing headlines dotted every gossip website on earth at the time his family was going through such an unspeakable tragedy. How could Marie have missed learning of it? Or perhaps she just hadn't made the connection. Although she'd find out soon enough.

"Yes, the needs of orphans are something dear to my family. What about you? How did you come to work for the APCF?"

She studied him before seeming to make a decision to answer frankly, "Without the support of the agency, I wouldn't be here. I'm an orphan myself."

Think before you speak, Marie reminded herself as she sipped her coffee opposite Zander at the table. There was something so open and inviting about his face it made her want to tell him about all of the things she'd learned to keep private.

He was the kind of man girls dreamed of. Not Marie, because she'd learned the hard way long ago never to dream. But somebody else's dream come true. A man with the power and know-how to bring ideas to life. To make yesterdays disappear and tomorrows look bright. In other words, he and those soulful almond-shaped eyes of his were dangerous. Because they could make a girl start to think about things that could never be.

"You're an orphan and now you work for the Alliance for Parentless Children of France," Zander said after putting the white porcelain coffee cup down onto its saucer. "You're exactly the reason we need the gala to be a resounding success. So that we can continue to assist parentless children all the way into adulthood."

She wasn't sure that she liked being discussed as if she was a case study students were analyzing at university. Although she was quite an example of everything that was wrong in society for orphaned children. With wounds she hoped no one would ever uncover. She'd rather die with them as memories covered in cobwebs that she kept in a tattered box in a corner of a never-visited attic. Unwrapping them only in private.

"The agency helped me get a job so I could go to university and then placed me in a position afterward."

"And event planning is where your passions lie?"

She wasn't sure why he was asking so many questions. Was he trying to determine whether she'd be able to assist him with his gala? Was he just asking out of idle inquiry? Or another motive? Fighting the urge to confide in him, she steadied herself. It wasn't often that anyone asked her about herself so she wasn't too savvy at it.

"Yes, I do like helping to bring all the pieces of an event together. Being part of a collaborative effort. Working with a team." Kind of like a family, she thought but didn't say. Because it hurt too much. "But we mainly do educational seminars and retreats. Rolls and coffee, sack lunches, that type of thing."

"Right." Zander checked his phone and with, apparently, nothing urgent there he placed it screen down on the table. "Okay, then, the first thing we need to do is announce the theme to the invitees."

Obviously, that was where his interest about her ended.

"We'll do a follow-up invitation as if we planned it that way all along," Marie offered.

"That's good. Like it was a secret we decided not to reveal right away. I want to go with some kind of costume or masquerade ball. It's classic. I think people enjoy disguising themselves with outfits and wigs so they can act with abandon. It's an innocent enough way for the guests to have a decadent evening."

"How do you have such insight into the psyche of the donors?" He surely seemed to know what he was doing.

"I've been going to charity events my entire life."

"Were your parents big donors?"

"You could say that. They made a lot of appearances."

"Oh, are they famous?"

"Something like that." He flagged the waiter. "Another café au lait, please. You?" he asked her.

"Yes, that would be nice, thank you."

Zander nodded at the waiter, who took his exit.

"A costume ball in and of itself isn't enough. We need to tell them what they're masquerading as."

Marie racked her brain. She wanted to make suggestions that Zander would like. She was in uncharted waters here. He was talking about balls the likes of which she'd never seen before. But that didn't matter—what did is that it would impress his guests.

"As I was saying earlier," he continued, "there's so much money in Cannes, especially this time of year. All of the Hollywood glitterati are here for the film festival and half of Europe is here to ogle them. Plus, the spring galas and balls are starting so everyone is expecting to part with their money. The APCF should be getting a bigger share of the bounty."

Knowing she was just blocks away from the ultraluxury hotels on La Croisette, where many of the rich and infamous stayed, Marie couldn't help but wonder about the lifestyles of the privileged class it seemed Zander was a part of.

What kind of care did these people take of their sons and daughters? Did they have happy homes, making sure their children felt loved and secure? Did they hug them close and protect them from harm? Or did they leave their care to others, without knowing if they were being treated right? Which type was Zander? How was he raised? Did he have children?

"Do you have children?" she couldn't help asking even though he had been cryptic when she pried into what he did for a living.

"You ask a lot of questions."

"Only the important ones."

That simply drew a chuckle from him, those dark-as-night eyes taking on a bit of glisten.

Which got her out of a tight spot. Because

she wasn't one to answer the big questions, so it wasn't fair of her to ask them.

Marie's heart thumped in double time to her steps on the way back to the office. Zander was simply the most stimulating company she'd ever been in! She'd never met anyone like him. He was so sure of himself and he had an unending stream of ideas to which he encouraged discussion. She actually felt a bit slow-witted around him, though she imagined it was his innate confidence that contributed to his panache.

Not to mention how stunning he was, with those piercing eyes that caught her every hesitation, every pause, every downward glance. He read right into her. He was going to be hard to hide from. And Marie had plenty to hide.

Once she settled in at the desk in her office, she speculated on how someone became a self-assured and successful person like Zander. With her parents long dead, and in working for the good of other orphans, Marie often found herself trying to analyze what kind of upbringing led to a fully functioning adult.

She knew that two people might have grown up with exactly the same opportunities yet one could become accomplished in both vocation and personal relationships. Whereas the other might succumb to crime, substance abuse, mental illness or some other type of marginalized existence. While upbringing was not a complete predictor of someone's future, it was a start.

Did Zander have a supportive childhood with parents who sheltered him when needed and encouraged risk when that was what was called for? She couldn't help but ponder about his background. Along with what it might be like to be held in his big, long arms, though she chastised herself for that inappropriate thought as soon as she had it. Yet she simply couldn't stop imagining being enveloped by him, swept into his sureness, giving her a sense of belonging her rootless past had never allowed.

Marie shook her head. Dashing Zander was the event chair for this very fancy benefit she found herself a part of. There wasn't to be anything personal between the two of them. Zander was a member of the upper class. Men like him didn't give a second glance to girls like her, who'd had it rough and were just scraping by. Money attracted money, confidence married confidence and so on. Wasn't that how it went? And what was she doing thinking about marrying anyway? Her love life thus far had just been links in a chain of the disappointment she had always known.

Starting with the top one, Marie moved the boxes that were on her desk and stacked them into a corner on the floor. She needed a workspace. Picking up the office phone with its many buttons, she called the front desk to find out what Felice's phone extension was. And left a message that she was available for the end-of-the-day meeting they'd agreed upon.

Before they parted Zander had asked her if she could continue working tonight and said that he'd send his driver at seven. So she'd need to finish up with Felice at the office and then go to her room to change into something more appropriate for the evening. Zander hadn't mentioned where his driver would be taking her.

After skimming through the files, Marie had a better sense of the agency's events. Some of the paperwork was from a year ago, some from five. It was a daunting prospect to have to sort through it all. She'd get to it as she could, but Felice had stressed to her that the gala was the number one priority.

Marie bit her lip, thinking again that being forced to spend lots of her time with Zander on this gala was one heck of a high-quality problem to have. Although she needed to tamp down her attraction to him, and fast!

"How did the meeting go?" Felice entered her office and closed the door. Marie looked up from the notes she was reviewing.

"Well, I think. He wants to meet with me again tonight to go into more detail."

"And you're available I hope?"

Marie bit back a snicker. Why wouldn't she be available? When she'd arrived this morning, she'd dropped off her suitcases and come straight to the office. And with no guarantees that she be promoted to the job permanently, she wouldn't even be giving up her room in Toulouse just yet. In short, Marie Paquet's life was in complete flux. Evening plans were the last thing on her mind.

"You'll need to devote yourself to Zander for the time being," Felice continued. The words *devote yourself to Zander* crawled down Marie's back, making her twitch in her seat. Devotion wasn't hard to imagine.

Perhaps there was already someone who had devoted herself to him. In fact, why on earth wouldn't there be? A smart and sophisticated man like him would surely have devotees lined up around the block. For all she knew, he was married or spoken for. Who was the Iris he had been talking to on the phone earlier today?

Regardless, Marie's task was to render this gala to everyone's satisfaction. Not to pry into Zander's relationship status.

"He talked to me about how extravagant he wants this to be. Something about being on par with the great balls of Venice. Do we have party vendors that can pull off something that ambitious?"

"This is Cannes," Felice assured. "This town knows how to throw a party better than most of the world. Of course, we have event partners up to the task."

Felice tapped into her phone. Once the ring began, she placed it on Marie's desk and hit the speaker button.

"Chef Jean Luc Malmond."

"Jean Luc, Felice here at the APCF."

"Felice, my sweet."

"We've had a bit of a staff shake-up here. And we're not entirely clear what has been settled upon for the gala's menu."

"Let me pull up my notes."

"And I have you on speakerphone with Marie Paquet, who will be our liaison for the event."

"A pleasure to meet you."

"You, too. On the phone, that is."

"As you know we have Zander de Nellay as event chair," Felice said to Jean Luc. "He wants to go lavish. I'm not sure Marie's predecessor had a grasp on the scale of the event."

"One thousand guests at the mansion," Marie added. That headcount was far larger than anything she'd ever worked on before. She was excited by the challenge. Among other things.

"I see we talked about starting with waiters passing hors d'oeuvres on trays during the cocktail hour," Jean Luc reported. "Then we seat the guests for a soup course. Followed by the entrée course with wine. Then a salad. Afterward, dessert buffets stationed at several locations in the ballroom. Continuous cocktail service in the great hall, ancillary salons and on the lawn."

"Do you have that, Marie?" Felice asked her across the desk. "You can discuss this with Zander when you meet with him tonight. See if he likes that basic outline."

"Got it."

"Jean Luc, I'm going to have Marie call you to set up a meeting this week."

"Yes, let's finalize as soon as possible. With the social season upon us, I'm like a decapitated chicken." Jean Luc let go of a laugh.

After they got off the phone, Felice helped Marie make a list of points to discuss with Zander when she saw him later.

Intrigue still nagged at Marie.

She sensed something a bit mysterious about Zander. For example, he never directly answered her innocent-enough query about what he did for work, saying only that he was affiliated with several charities.

"Felice, what does Zander do for a living?"

"Do?" Felice looked at her like she had just arrived from Mars. Marie wanted to impress the director by having all the information, but nothing in the notes said anything specifically about that. "You mean other than his royal duties?"

"Royal duties?" Marie's shoulders arched back.

"Marie, His Highness Zander de Nellay is a prince. He's the son of His Serene Highness Prince Hugh and Princess Claudine of Charlegin."

Marie's fists opened and closed. She'd just had lunch at an outdoor café with a prince? Obviously, a poor orphan from the meanest streets in North Marseilles had never met a member of royalty before.

She'd seen enough of the royals who were always on television and in magazines to know that they didn't wear regalia and crowns every time they were seen in public. Still, there was nothing about Zander, nor had he said anything, to give her any indication that he was a prince.

A prince!

"Felice, I didn't know. It wasn't anywhere in Jic's paperwork." Although she remembered in a handwritten note Jic had doodled a crown above Zander's name. Hardly a clear communiqué, but now it made sense.

"I assumed you knew, therefore it never occurred to me to mention it."

She'd be working on this gala with a prince! Why hadn't he told her who he was? It seemed like he went out of his way not to mention it.

When she saw him tonight, should she tell him that she'd only just found out? Or should she let it remain unspoken as if it was something she'd already known? Nothing in her previous reference taught her protocol for this sort of thing.

"His Highness Prince Zander de Nellay of Charlegin." Marie said it out loud to try it on for size. He'd mentioned his homeland but not that his family were the rulers there!

"It's a small principality reigned over by a prince rather than a king. Surely you heard the news a year ago when Zander's sister, Elise, who was the crown princess, and her husband were killed in a plane crash?"

Once Felice began to explain, Marie vaguely remembered hearing about that tragedy on the news. At the time she hadn't heard of Charlegin and had forgotten all about it. Royal comings and goings were of no interest to her. But she recalled the photo that had been shown on the news of Elise, a beautiful woman who, now that Marie thought about it, had those dark almond-shaped eyes the same as Zander.

"Is there a specific reason the prince is affiliated with the APCF and chairing our gala?"

"Alain really didn't fill you in, did he? Princess Elise and her husband, Prince Valentin, had a baby girl. She was left an orphan. Zander has taken her in. Princess Abella de Nellay is the next heir to the Charlegin throne."

CHAPTER THREE

MARIE WALKED DOWN the corridor to the room she was staying in. When Alain had described the facility as "nothing fancy," he hadn't been kidding. The carpet was a worn gray and the white walls were cold. He'd told her the building was a multipurpose center for the APCF, providing temporary shelter to orphans in foster care who were, perhaps, being relocated and awaiting placement. Or to those who needed to be removed from bad situations but before new arrangements could be made.

A chill swept through her at the memory, several memories in fact, of herself being in those circumstances. When frightened children were grouped together in nondescript locations to, essentially, sit around and wait to see where they were going to live next. Often fearful that as bad as their previous placement might have been, what awaited them in the future could be worse.

While there were many generous and compassionate people in the world who became foster parents, Marie hadn't had the luck to be placed with any of them. Uniformly, the six overcrowded and dirty apartments she'd been sent to over the years were habitats with adults who should not have been entrusted with the care of children.

Her parents had been no better suited. Marie had never been part of a healthy, living and breathing family. The kind she used to dream about, where people helped each other through the hard times and enjoyed each other's successes. An adult now, she'd long accepted that was never to be for her.

At twenty-five, Marie was on her own. The past might forever haunt her, but the future was hers to make or break.

The key to her room's door stuck as she pushed it into the lock and it took a couple of jimmies to fit it in. Her two suitcases were exactly where she had left them this morning after her train ride from Toulouse.

A single-sized bed with an unpainted wood nightstand beside it and a table with an armchair were the only furnishings. Sparse, institutional but clean. Time would tell whether she was in Cannes to stay, and if so, she'd look for a small place she could personalize.

At least this would be a private space to think in, and her phone and the laptop Felice had given her would allow her to work and communicate as needed.

In fact, she pulled the laptop out of her bag and brought it with her as she kicked off her shoes and sat down on the bed. She propped her back against the wall and set the computer on her knees. Logging on to the internet, she had business to take care of. Research, anyway.

Into the search field she typed "Prince Zander de Nellay." Dozens of links popped up. She clicked to the first one, *Single Hot Royals*, even though the name sounded like a gossip site that may or may not contain anything true.

An hour and many websites later, she had gathered plenty of reconnaissance. Firstly, Prince Zander was incapable of taking a bad photo. Whether snapped in a tuxedo at official occasions, socializing in a tailored suit worn without a tie or on the golf course in well-fitted sportswear, the man was simply gorgeous.

Next, unsurprisingly, he had been associated romantically with several beautiful and famous women. Marie found photos of him from all over the world, either vacationing in tropical paradises or in the thick of pulsing cities, with stunning females on his arm. With an American movie star on a sailboat in the Caribbean. Riding horseback in the countryside with a London fashion model. At an Italian opera house with a Chinese ballerina.

One thing was consistent about Marie's online detective work. There were few pictures of Zander taken in the past year, other than at charitable or royal functions. After his sister and her husband died, Zander all but went into hiding. As Felice had told her that he was now the one caring for his baby niece, his absence from the party scene was understandable.

Although about six months ago, when he had been photographed he'd always had the same eight-foot-tall stick insect on his arm. A glamazon named Henriette Fontaine. Three months later, he'd made the same appearances alone. Marie's detective work added up to a conclusion that Zander was heterosexual and unmarried.

Wanting a few minutes to ready herself before she met with him again, Marie closed the laptop. She opened her suitcases and hung her limited and plain wardrobe in the room's one closet. Not sure what to wear for the evening, she flipped through her options.

He hadn't specified where they were going. So it wasn't a dinner invitation, yet it wasn't a business meeting. A suit would be wrong, but one of her few dressier dresses wouldn't be right, either.

A quick glance in the mirror on the closet door was a blaring reminder that she needed a haircut. Obviously, she wasn't planning to move to Cannes, where absolutely everyone had a "yacht chic" style that must have cost them a fortune. How would she have known that a haircut was urgent? And in her wildest dreams she couldn't have known that she'd be interacting with a prince and had to consider what to wear to spend the evening with him.

Deciding on the best middle ground she could think of, she put on a black pencil skirt with black flats. But she dressed it up with a shiny red blouse—not real silk, of course—that had a low neckline with a bow detail. Hair swept into a twist and the pearl earrings that she'd saved for a year to buy, she hoped she looked respectable. This wasn't a date, Marie kept reminding herself as she applied a bit of makeup to try to cover up the telltale signs of her very long day. She hadn't been on a date in a long time. Two years ago, in fact.

Gerard.

Marie had been on casual dates with a few men and had one boyfriend. Gerard was fifth generation of a farming family. He frequently came into Toulouse for banking and supplies, and they met at a brasserie close to the AP-CF's office there.

Gerard took a liking to her. Or so it seemed. Attending a sporting event or movie together, Marie thought they were at ease with each other. She didn't have a lot of friends so she appreciated Gerard's companionship. While there were warning signs from the very beginning, she shoved them aside. For a few months, she convinced herself she was happy.

But when she went with him to meet his parents, they didn't welcome her with open arms. They asked a lot of questions. She'd learned to say as little as possible about her past because people seemed to always judge her by it. Not leaving it as a mystery, they took it upon themselves to do some research. And once they found out about her, that was that. No son of theirs was going to be with a girl left orphaned by criminals. Think of the gene pool. They saw to it that the relationship didn't last long.

Gerard didn't protest. Obviously, Marie hadn't meant enough to him to defend her to his parents. No one had ever fought for her. She didn't think anyone ever would.

Yet now she was making up her face for her meeting with a prince. The juxtaposition gave her hope. People never really knew where their road would take them.

Something she did know was that she was only herself. With her checkered upbringing and her emotional scars. If she was ever to be with a man again, which she highly doubted anyway, it would have to be somebody who accepted and even loved her for who she was.

Although that was all speculation. Marie had no intention of getting into any kind of relationship with anyone again. She'd had enough hurt, neglect, betrayal and disappointment to last a lifetime. There was only one person she could count on, who had her best interests at heart.

Herself.

With a click on her purse's buckle, she left to meet the striking gala chairman who just happened to be a prince.

The buzz of the doorbell snapped Zander's attention from his paperwork. A glance down to his phone informed him it was later than he'd realized. It was time for Marie's arrival.

It had been a long day with moving into

the apartment and his visit to the APCF, but there was more work ahead. While Marie was pleasant, not to mention attractive, she was not educated on the requirements for the gala. He couldn't do this alone so hoped to get her caught up quickly.

"Come in." Zander opened the door wide for her to enter.

He noticed that she had gussied herself up for the evening. The hair that had been rather adorably a mess at lunch was now pulled sleekly back. The sparkle of the round blue eyes was set off by a shade of pink lipstick that brought focus to her small and perfectly shaped mouth.

A lovely young woman had come calling. And it took Zander aback.

Until he reminded who he was, who she was, and that she had only come to work.

"Oh, my gosh!" Marie seemed to be startled as soon as she passed into the apartment. She countered with, "I mean, how nice, your…"

He waited while she took in the full panorama of the spacious living room with its solid wall of sliding glass doors leading to the terrace and the sea view beyond.

With the doors slid fully open, a twilight breeze billowed the white gauzy curtains. Inside, the blond wood combined with fabrics in shades of soothing taupes and grays gave the furniture a calm feel amid the opulence of the room. There was no denying that it was a spectacular residence.

"May I ask, is this where you live?"

"Yes, why?" That wasn't the first time Marie had blurted out a direct question that someone might consider private and not to be asked in casual conversation. He found her bluntness refreshing. People hardly ever let their thinking show when they were around His Highness Prince Zander.

"I just wasn't sure if you… I mean you can obviously affor…"

"Yes?" He folded his arms across his chest, waiting.

"You mentioned that you were only here for the season."

This exchange reinforced why he'd gotten into the habit of not introducing himself by his title to everyone he met. Marie was falling over her words just thinking of him as a wealthy philanthropist. One could only imagine how she'd act once she knew she was in the presence of a prince and a baby heir to the throne.

"Yes." He couldn't help playing along a little longer.

"I've never seen...well, what would I know? I've never been to Cannes before. It's very glamorous, isn't it?"

"For centuries now."

"I hope that if I get the job with the APCF permanently I can find an apartment in my price range. Not that you'd...well, you know what I mean."

True, Zander had never been concerned with, or even knowledgeable of, how much a rental property cost to lease. He got the feeling Marie was well versed on the subject.

She had told him that she herself had been orphaned and that the agency had helped her. He wondered what hardships she had endured, financial or otherwise. Something unspoken about her told him that there were probably a lot.

As pretty as she was, he didn't find it hard to imagine her as a scruffy cliché of an orphan. Through the APCF he'd learned about orphaned children all over the world. Some were left parentless as a result of war or natural disasters, or freak accidents as Abella was. Others were due to the consequences of illness, poverty, suicide, addiction or crime. He had no idea how Marie had become orphaned or what her road to adulthood had been. And was more curious than he expected to be.

When they'd parted this afternoon with an agreement to reconvene tonight, he'd planned on taking her out for a working dinner. But when he arrived home, the baby was sleeping, and Iris was extremely tired and asked if he'd mind her leaving. Of course, he had his driver ferry her to the small flat he'd leased for her for their time in Cannes.

Which meant that meeting here with Marie was the only option. One he wasn't exactly comfortable with. He'd learned the hard way that he needed to shelter Abella from strangers as much as possible.

"Can I offer you a drink?" Zander asked absentmindedly, sidetracked by a peep he heard coming from the baby monitor. Perhaps Abella was waking.

"Just water, please."

Hearing no further stirring from the baby, Zander poured two waters and gestured for Marie to join him at the sofas. They sat opposite each other.

"Let's start by talking through the gala in order of its components."

"Okay." Marie opened the folder she had brought along.

"Guests arrive via limousine or personal drivers," he began. "Do we have valets for cars that need to be parked?"

"Yes, I see here we have contracted with a company for that."

"Good. The guests exit their cars and proceed to the red carpet."

"Red carpet?" Marie tilted her head. "For the APCF fund-raiser?"

"That's how it's done. I've got prominent businesspeople coming, celebrities, members of royal families." He murmured the last example quickly as if it were an afterthought. "We're looking for maximum exposure. The press will be out in force to photograph the arrivals on the carpet. The gowns. The jewelry. And so on."

He meant what he said. Once his staff had put out the news that Prince Zander was hosting the gala, the royal-watching media had taken interest. Which was the plan, because all publicity would serve to raise awareness about the APCF.

While Zander wasn't among the royals whose antics made constant headlines, he found it curious that Marie didn't recognize him at all. Leveraging his position and power was how he was able to assist a number of high-profile causes. Not only was it what royals throughout history had done, it was something that made him feel good. The benevolent work was a way to pay back for the luxury and advantages that were bestowed on him as his birthright.

"So I'll need to order an actual red carpet?" she asked after a sip of her drink.

"For a costume ball, I was thinking of a black carpet. We'll light it just so, and make it mysterious and sexy."

"Sexy?" Marie clasped and unclasped her fists a few times. "Are the struggles of orphans sexy?"

"Point taken. But, yes, hidden identities and checkbooks filled with lots and lots of money are sexy."

Good heavens, Marie was not like any woman he'd ever met before! Granted, the orbit he operated in wasn't filled with ordinary people leading typical lives. The women he knew ate, slept and breathed money. They knew where it was and how to get a piece of it. And they surely knew how to spend it.

What was he going to do with this innocent Marie? As he watched that sensual mouth of hers take another sip of her drink, he thought of a few things. And then promptly reprimanded himself! Women were no longer on his agenda.

He'd get used to Marie and then she wouldn't be so fascinating. Which was reinforced when he heard another blip from the baby monitor. The sound came from the only female who mattered in his life, a position she would hold for the foreseeable future. Abella was awake and would soon want to be retrieved from her crib.

"One photo stop on the carpet should be a flower wall," Zander continued. "That's great for photos."

"What's a flower wall?" Marie leaned forward a bit, unintentionally giving Zander a nice view of the creamy skin of her neck.

On the coffee table between them sat the stack of invitations to the various balls, fundraisers and parties that would kick off the social season. He remembered that he'd instructed an assistant to RSVP for two to all of them, that Prince Zander would be bringing a plus one. He'd still yet to figure out who that was going to be.

But to walk into one of those events without a drop-dead gorgeous woman on his arm was like to appear with a target on his back. Every female gold digger on the continent would find her way to him before the season was up, feigning interest about the baby and trying to finagle an invitation to spend time with her. Just as Henriette had a few months ago.

He needed to come up with a trustworthy

female friend who could accompany him to these events so he didn't have to dodge the unwanted advances. Perhaps one of his late sister's friends, one who knew the family and wouldn't have any ulterior motives.

No, he mused, memories of Elise were the last thing he wanted. The flourishing constant reminder of her untimely death was in the very next room, haunting him every day.

Abella began to make so many cooing sounds from her room that Marie glanced over to the baby monitor.

Even though Marie was with the APCF, and didn't seem at all like the opportunist women he had known, he'd hadn't planned on inviting her to the apartment. At least not yet. But since they'd be working together closely and frequently, a proposition that filled him with a trickle of eager anticipation, he surely couldn't keep the baby a secret.

Although he took a split second to hope he wasn't making a mistake. Like his recent one, which still filled him with remorse.

When Zander stood, Marie looked unclear as to whether she was supposed to stay seated or to get up, as well. "Please, be comfortable. If you'll pardon me a moment. I'll be right back."

"Uh, okay."

"If you recall, at lunch today you asked me what connection I had to the needs of parentless children. I'm going to show you."

He wasn't able to read Marie's expression as he excused himself and made his way down the hall to Abella's room, gently opening the door that he had left ajar.

"Da." Abella recognized Zander's presence despite the room being in darkness. That she kept calling him *Da* was a problem he still hadn't figured out how to solve.

Flicking on the muted light that was contained inside a pink-and-blue unicorn lamp, he was greeted by his niece's exuberant face. "Uncle Zander is here, Bell-bell. Do you want to get up?"

"Uppie."

When he returned to the living room with Abella, Marie stood.

"This little miracle is my catalyst for concern about children left orphaned. Marie, I'd like you to meet…"

"Her Highness Crown Princess Abella de Nellay of Charlegin," Marie interrupted. "Heir to the throne."

"You *do* know who I am?" Zander's brow furrowed at the confusion. Abella nuzzled her face against his neck, filling him with that almost all-consuming need to don a suit of armor and do her bidding. While he'd convinced himself that Marie couldn't possibly be the enemy, someone's motives might not be evident at first. He was responsible for this baby, and he'd put her first in any situation. "Why didn't you say so?"

"I didn't know until Felice filled me in this afternoon. Why didn't you mention it, Your Highness? Am I supposed to call you Your Highness?"

Of course Felice had filled Marie in on his identity. The agency was planning to take full advantage of having a member of a royal family serve as the gala event chair. He'd only played along this afternoon because it seemed like Marie didn't know. And that had given him a chance to get a little bit of insight into her before the throne-and-scepter bit had her stumbling around him like she was now.

"You surely do not have to call me Your Highness or any such address unless we're in company where it's appropriate. By all means continue to call me Zander."

"Want bottie," Abella voiced her request.

While Marie watched on, he poured fresh water into Abella's cup. He and the baby still referred to it as a bottie even though she had progressed to lidded sippy cups. He was grateful for the activity as a distraction from Marie's fierce stare. She was hurt that he hadn't identified himself properly and was using that glare to fight back.

"Please, sit down again." He gestured for Marie to sit opposite him.

Abella eagerly sucked on the nozzle of her drink.

"She's...so...beautiful." The words tripped out of Marie's mouth as she looked affectionately at the baby princess.

Zander's thick fingers lightly brushed Abella's hair backward out of her face as she drank her water. "Yes, she is."

As Abella squirreled around on his lap, Zander adjusted to accommodate her movements. Straightening one leg and bending the other, then reversing when something else caught the baby's eye. The two of them were in perpetual motion.

"May I ask again, was there a purpose in your not telling me who you were when clearly I didn't know?"

"I'm sorry, Marie," he said sincerely despite the constant shifting. "So often when I meet people in an official capacity, they don't talk to me as if I was of the same species. They feel they have to treat me with formal-ity, and then before you know it, they're falling all over themselves."

Marie repeatedly smoothed her bangs down on her forehead, seeming uncomfortable and making Zander feel awful.

"Since, obviously, you'd discover my title soon enough," he continued, "I was trying to use the time for us to get acquainted, just person to person."

"So I was your guinea pig?"

"I apologize that must be how it seems to you. Can you forgive me?"

Marie looked around, again taking in the view beyond the terrace. She glanced down to the plush white carpeting. Studied the crystal glass that held her beverage. As if she was fully fathoming that it was a prince's water she was drinking.

All the sorts of things Zander hated. He flashed back to the last time he was with Henriette. They'd traveled to a luxurious parador in Spain for a long weekend. The way she had inspected the bed sheets and bathroom towels was just embarrassing. Zander figured whenever he left her sight, the girl was probably looking up their monetary value online.

While he didn't suspect that anything like that was going through Marie's mind, he hated that everything, including a simple

drinking glass, was how people were catego-
rized, labeled and judged.

He had a great responsibility on his head,
in Abella's well-being. Henriette had been a
call to arms and he'd become quickly adept
at keeping people at bay. While there were
bodyguards and royal handlers in Charlegin assigned to Abella, Zander thought of
her safety as his own particular job, and one
he took seriously. He'd encountered other
women like Henriette who acted like they
cared about the baby when really they were
angling as to what *pretending* to care about
the baby could gain them. Zander was making sure to have no more of that.

Marie chose her next words deliberately. "I
do understand a little bit about what you're
talking about. People find out facts about you
and then they make assumptions."

Which led Zander to certainty that there
was more she could say but chose not to. "It
sounds like you've had personal experience
with that."

Marie was clearly holding something back.
Even though he believed from the pit of his
stomach that she meant no harm, he'd be sure
not to leave her alone with the baby. Once he
got to know her better, he'd reassess. After

all, she did work for the APCF and Felice assured him he was in good hands.

For now, though, the metal shield was across his chest. This was his new life.

"Let's get back to the task at hand," Zander said after succeeding in getting Abella occupied beside him with a set of plastic blocks, and more than ready to move on from the discussion of his royal status.

Abella accidently knocked her sippy cup to the floor. Marie reached down to pick it up.

"I've got it," Zander quickly blipped and snatched it from Marie's hand. Her surprised look made him aware that his action was overly defensive. What would be the harm in Marie touching something of Abella's? But was there such a thing as being *too* careful when it came to the protection of the crown princess?

In any case, should he apologize or just ignore it? Odd that he was second-guessing himself left and right around Marie.

"We were talking about the red carpet."

"Black carpet," Marie corrected, regrouping.

"The VIP guests walk the carpet, the press is out in force, etcetera."

"What about the attendees who are not, as

you call them, VIP? Do they come in through the sewage system?"

Zander laughed. He couldn't help but like this woman. Her frankness and spunk were riveting. "It does sound horribly undemocratic, I know. But the reality is that the press is only interested in famous names and faces. Bringing publicity to the APCF is our goal. We have to keep our sights on that."

"No problem," she insisted with a defiantly jutted chin, then made some notes. "This is just more gala than the galas we've done before. I'm looking forward to it."

Zander glanced over again to those party invitations on the table. An idea circulated around and around his brain. Until it started to take shape and make sense.

Many birds could be killed with one stone, as the saying went. If he was going to get Marie to fathom the elaborate kind of evening he was planning for the APCF, it would be invaluable if she could see some of them unfold. He could take her along as his date for the engagements in the first few weeks of the season. Then she'd have firsthand knowledge of not one but several event styles. She'd see Cannes at its heights, when the whole city rose to the occasion of these legendary parties.

Secondly, with a woman accompanying him the pressure would be off. It wasn't hard to imagine Marie in designer gowns and with her hair and makeup styled to perfection. She'd be a fetching date and would surely ward off the hangers-on who usually planted themselves in Zander's path.

Plus it would give him and Marie an opportunity to spend plenty of time together and develop a good working relationship.

It was a genius scheme that would work on every level. Zander mentally confirmed his decision and was quite pleased with himself for thinking of it.

Almost. There was only one thing gnawing in his craw as he looked to Marie sitting opposite, with Abella still happily playing next to him. There was something about Marie that was a little too intriguing. Alluring even. Which could lead to trouble.

He could get past it, though. Between Henriette's burn that still smarted, his feelings for the baby and the massive amount of specifics to take care of for the event, he wouldn't have time for anything else.

It was a perfect plan. Wasn't it?

Marie's sweet blue eyes watched the baby play. She smiled at moments then went wide-eyed when Abella displayed her proficiency with the blocks. "Great job, Abella," she blurted at one point.

Most definitely not like the women he knew.

Her cheap shiny red blouse reminded him of her wildly windblown hair at lunch today. He'd have to buy her gowns and shoes and whatnot to attend these parties where only the finest would do.

"Marie," he said finally, after staring at her for a long while he'd thought through all the particulars. "You're going to attend some black-tie events with me in the next couple of weeks. You'll need evening wear."

CHAPTER FOUR

"I'VE NEVER WORN anything like this." The words stuttered out of Marie's mouth as she looked at herself in the shop's three-way mirror. The underslip of the midnight-blue gown fit her like a glove. It was topped by a chiffon layer to which a thousand matching crystals were affixed.

Of course, she didn't know if it was really a thousand. She only knew it was the right number of beads, not so many that the dress became flashy or over the top. No, this was subtle elegance of the kind Marie had not only never tried on but never even seen up close. She could imagine a dozen workers crafting to create this gown.

"The blue is lovely on you," Zander voted in.

Flushed by his flattery, Marie ran her hand along the scooped neckline of the dress. Its needlework and seams were expertly hidden. The inner layer felt smooth against the delicate skin of her décolleté. With a slight tug to the thin straps, she lifted the bodice of the gown a bit higher for modesty. As quietly and quickly as a stealth weapon, Pati the sales manager, a tiny woman with arthritic fingers, pinned the straps to Marie's satisfaction.

"Thank you, Pati." Zander acknowledged her handiwork.

"Perhaps you'd like to wear your hair up with this gown," Pati suggested. "May I?"

Marie allowed Pati to lift her hair with a few clips to see how it would look. With the low cut of the dress's front and her hair out of the way, Marie's neck looked tall and stately. An unfamiliar description.

A couple of Marie's coworkers in Toulouse were into clothes and always encouraging her to dress more daringly or trendily. She paid them no mind. Having spent most of her life not knowing whether she'd even have clean clothes for school the next day, fashion was the furthest thing from young Marie's mind.

As an adult, she'd settled into practical and inexpensive pieces. It rarely occurred to her to replace or add to her current wardrobe unless something was so worn it would appear unprofessional. On the rare occasions she did shop, it was surely not at a store like the one they were in now.

The boutique carried formal wear from both world-renowned and local designers. Once again reminding Marie that she was in the French Riviera where sun and money informed the lifestyle. If she got the job at the APCF permanently, it would all take some getting used to.

She'd no doubt need to find her place on the *other side of the tracks*, as the saying went. Just as her ex-boyfriend, Gerard, never hesitated to remind her, she should keep her expectations low. But hopefully, there would be somewhere she could afford to live in a working-class neighborhood. Maybe she'd meet some people there. The La Croisette crowd was not her kind. Never were and never would be.

In fact, the combination of trying on the gown coupled with Prince Zander's observant eye was overwhelming. The way he looked at her was nothing like Gerard, or any other man, had. He'd picked her up earlier this morning, after deciding last night that she'd accompany him to some of the swanky fundraisers that were on his calendar. And presto, with a snap of his fingers, she was suddenly shopping in Cannes and living in a different universe. One she could hardly fathom.

To pull off the magnitude of event Zander wanted to for the APCF, Marie was going to need an education on how events of that scale were mounted. She was grateful for the prince's invitation, although intimidated to move in a social circle she knew nothing about. Joining him for some hands-on learning was an opportunity there'd be no substitute for.

"Zander." Marie moved from the three-sided mirror over to the settee where he was sitting. She waited until Pati was well out of earshot before asking, "I appreciate your confidence in me but… I don't know how to say this…isn't it kind of obvious that I'm not the type of woman who would go to a ball on a prince's arm?"

"What kind of woman would that be?" He leaned back in his seat, legs parted as he scratched his chin.

"Don't you have well…people you live among?"

"Have you been talking to my mother?" he joked.

Although his smile was flirty, Marie pressed on.

"But aren't you supposed to be seen with women from your…planet?"

"And you're not?"

Perhaps he didn't know what a hot-button issue like belonging was to someone like Marie. Whose parents weren't capable of creating a nurturing home for a child. And who, after they died when she was eleven, was tossed from one foster home to the next. And mercilessly teased, ridiculed for being homeless and rootless. Never being around people she trusted or felt accepted by. No one to catch her if she fell or celebrate her when she thrived. Although she was doing great by any standards in her adult life, those weren't scars that ever healed.

If Zander thought she was just as good as the selective crowd his life was built around, why did he grab Abella's sippy cup out of her hands last night as if she was infected with the bubonic plague? She could appreciate that he might not like Abella's things to be handled by strangers, but his actions surely spoke louder than his words.

Noticing that she was flustered, Zander said, "First of all, I'll bring whomever I want to a party and dare anyone to tell me otherwise." More words. "Secondly, you look fabulous, and chic, in that gown. You're not going to be wearing a sign on your back that tells everyone how much money your father makes."

"I'm an orphan. My father doesn't make anything."

"Forgive me, yes, I know that. It was just meant as a figure of speech."

"But do you think…"

He reached out and took Marie's hand. His was so solid and sturdy, tingles tracked down her body at his touch. Her neck and throat, exposed in the gown, must have turned beet red. She didn't know if she was really going to be able to hold herself together. Not only was this entire shopping expedition way out of her frame of reference, Zander himself was too much. He awakened something in her. She was hyperaware of herself in his presence and analyzing his every move.

As she had learned in counseling, when life became too much to bear Marie knew to deepen her breathing. After intaking plenty of extra oxygen, she was able to hear the words Zander spoke while he held her hand.

"This is a good idea, to give you first-hand knowledge of how these events are done. And I'll tell you something else. If you're going to stay in Cannes, I suggest you get comfortable mingling with the hoi polloi here. This is a moneyed town, full of people who have it and more who want it. An effective fund-raiser knows how to swing in the right circles."

"Yes, you're right, of course."

Pati moved toward them holding a couple of bottles of water. "Why don't we get you out of that dress and into another. Can I offer you a drink while you're changing? This, or a coffee?"

"I'd better take the dress off first!"

"Indeed." Pati turned to Zander. "Your Highness, we'll be right back."

"Zander."

Pati bowed her head. "Yes, Your Highness."

"Zander is fine, really," he said with a smirk.

Marie was completely taken aback by his warmth and humor as she followed Pati. Whatever preconceptions she might have had about the reserve of royalty was quickly being thrown out the window. But she had to caution herself not to read anything into his friendly demeanor.

A prince was never going to spend his time with the likes of her other than for the sake of his own goals, so it would be dangerous to get close to him. He had a means to an end and she was here only to serve him. That his ultimate aim was to bring as much money into the APCF as possible was certainly noble. And, she had to admit, added to his charm.

Not to mention those almond-shaped eyes that were always watching. There were those defined lips. Her eyes rolled back in her head when she allowed herself a split second of imagining what his mouth might feel like on her bare neck. Then there was that physique of his that today looked so taut under the tailored pink shirt and black jeans he was wearing. It might be heaven on earth to be in his embrace.

Pati ushered Marie back into the dressing area. Dressing *room*, singular, was the right word for it, as it was about the size of the bedroom Marie would be staying in. The walls were covered in textured wallpaper with black velvet fleurs-de-lis in a pattern. A black dais stood in the center of the room for pinning alterations.

There were mirrors everywhere. Antique armchairs upholstered in gold taffeta were arranged in a couple of groupings. Gowns on rolling racks were placed just so, as to not touch each other. A tall shoe stand with many rungs could accommodate a dozen pair. A glass case held evening bags and hair accessories. Marie had never given any thought to what a dressing room in a shop like this would look like, but it was magical.

With Pati's help, Marie stepped carefully out of the first gown. Sipping from the bottle of water, she felt uneasy seeing herself in all the mirrors with her low-cost cotton underwear amid the finery of the shop.

"The prince is very handsome, isn't he?" Pati stated rather than asked as she brought out the next dress for Marie to try.

"He is at that."

"And are you a…friend of his?"

As discreet as the manager of a designer shop in Cannes was expected to be, apparently even Pati couldn't resist prying out any data she could on Zander's relationship status. *It must be awful for him*, Marie thought to herself. People foisting themselves onto him not out of any genuine like but for self-centered reasons. In a funny way, she felt protective toward him.

"We're colleagues," she said flatly.

Marie's modeling the pewter-colored gown with the train got a "Yes!" from Zander when Pati brought her out to show him. "That will be perfect for the reception at the Carlsmon." He'd mentioned that they'd be attending a screening and party during the film festival at a hotel that was known as one of the centers of the action.

With Zander ten steps ahead of everyone else, as seemed to always be the case, he'd obviously contacted Pati ahead of time to explain what clothes Marie would need. And he was here with her making sure the selections were to his satisfaction. Marie wondered what typical days were like for His Highness, as a prince, a philanthropist and a royal baby's guardian.

Did he have an office somewhere that he reported to daily? A staff? Was it in Charlegin? Paris? With all his traversing of the world, she supposed a physical office would be impractical, not to mention unnecessary with today's technology. She considered how much about his lifestyle might have changed after the crown princess was put in his care.

Marie had to stand up very straight and force her shoulders back to wear the pewter dress properly. It was a gown for a confident woman, bold in its fit that left nothing to the imagination. It had halter-style straps with a V neckline. Under the bustline were two triangular cutouts that exposed bare skin. The geometric cutouts were echoed in the back. That little bit of skin peeking through was uncharacteristically daring for Marie. She was surprised at how much she loved it.

Having never walked in a gown with a train before, Marie got a quick course on how not to trip on the extra fabric.

"Thatta girl," Zander approved of her new posture. "You look just like one of the Hollywood stars who will be at the party."

Although Marie tried to breathe her heartbeat into not pounding, she feared it was. In a gown that probably cost more than she made in a month, Marie was going to a soiree where movie stars would be in attendance. That a girl from the *quartier nord*, as the worst streets of North Marseilles were called, with parents like hers and with the parade of incompetents who defined her adolescence after they were killed, was standing here today was unbelievable.

"Pati, what are we envisioning for the Laublie Foundation breast cancer research benefit? The theme is 'A Night in Mexico' and the dress is Mexican black tie," Zander declared and snapped Marie out of what could have had her looking back on a dark road.

"Your Highness—" Pati began.

"Zander."

"Zander," Pati finally managed with a

cough, "I was thinking of black lace with some added color. May I show you what I had in mind?"

Back in the dressing room, nothing could have prepared Marie for the next dress Pati brought out, explaining that it was made from antique black lace. Marie touched the exceptional fabric, and thought it was romantic and current and timeless all at once. She couldn't believe her eyes. Her heart fluttered when Pati zipped her into it.

The fitted bodice was sleeveless with a sweetheart neckline. It skimmed her torso down to her waist. On top of the lace in a diagonal from the décolleté on the left to beyond the waistline on the right was a swath of brightly colored hand-embroidered flowers. Yellow, red, green, blue and purple against black added up to making this a dress Marie could not have imagined existed. With the help of several petticoats underneath, the skirt portion poufed out and extended to floor length.

It was a ball gown of the highest order.

Marie's jaw dropped at her visage in the mirror as Pati slipped her feet into black high-heeled sandals with a red leather bow on each. Somehow little girl dress-up had become a reality.

Prince Charming included.

As a warning, though, she shook her head at her own reflection in the mirror. There was no prince to be hers. She was only doing the job she'd been asked to, which, bizarrely, entailed wearing these exquisite clothes.

A shiver shot through her as she realized that if Zander knew any details about her, about her parents, he wouldn't want her on his arm or anywhere near him. Or near Abella. Marie hated constantly dragging her past along with her wherever she went. How she wished to not be limited by it any longer.

For now, it was all professionalism. Detached. Reveal nothing of herself. That was all she had to do. And to keep her attraction to Zander in check.

To complete this gown's look, Pati gave Marie a pair of red satin gloves that extended past her elbows. "For that dramatic effect," Pati chirped. "And perhaps a necklace. With His Highness's approval, of course."

"Oh, my goodness." Marie couldn't help but skim one hand along the other arm to experience the shiny glide of the gloves. She surely hoped Zander liked this outfit because she knew it was the most beautiful she would ever wear as long as she lived.

* * *

After they'd finished at the dress shop, Zander led Marie toward La Croisette.

"Where are we going now?"

"Let's walk down to the beach."

He craved the sea breezes. Iris was still with Abella so he could afford a little more time out.

Zander directed them to an exclusive beach club where his family had year-round access.

"These beaches are private?" Marie exclaimed. "How is the ocean only available to certain people?"

Although he chuckled, he could grasp how strange this must all seem to her, as it would to the majority of people in the world. "Beach clubs, ball season, the film festival, Cannes can seem like another galaxy. Are you still game for taking this rocket ship with me?"

He'd noticed her habit of opening and closing her fists, which she was doing at the moment. "This is a once-in-a-lifetime chance for me to see Cannes through your eyes. I've never been on a private beach before."

"If you're going to get good at creating fund-raisers that bring in the big-money players, you should be inside their circle."

At the entrance, an attendant quickly greeted Zander. "Welcome, Your Highness.

Will you be dining or in need of sporting equipment?"

"No, thank you, and you can call me Zander. We're just having a quick stroll on the beach today."

"I'll have towels and chairs for you immediately."

The afternoon had turned to dusk as they walked the length of the club's boardwalk, past the outdoor restaurant and cocktail bar, the lounge chairs and yellow-and-white-striped umbrellas set in precise rows.

Sun worshippers had begun to pull clothing over their tiny bathing suits to make their way up toward the cafés and hotels that lined the Croisette. They'd have their cocktails and change into their evening finery, emerging after dark for whatever plans were on their agenda in this fantasyland of a beach town.

"Do you want to take your shoes off and walk in the sand?" Marie asked.

"Absolutely." The way she asked thrilled him, like he was a mischievous schoolboy who was supposed to be in class but had snuck out for a short taste of freedom.

She quickly kicked her off her sandals. Zander untied his oxfords, removed his socks and cuffed his pants a couple of turns up his leg. Of course, he had fashionable beachwear back at the penthouse but they were here now, spontaneity not something Zander typically had much of. They stepped down from the boardwalk into the soft, warm sand, flashing each other a clandestine nod.

"See," she said, "even a prince can set his toes free sometimes, can't he?"

He felt his grin spread from ear to ear.

An attendant magically appeared to lay a stack of thick towels down onto a couple of loungers for their return.

"Even if he has to have his own private beach," she kidded.

As they walked toward the sparkling blue water, Zander found himself with a yearning he couldn't quite put his finger on.

There was something so genuine about Marie. It touched his heart.

Certainly the shopping excursion was a feast for the eyes, watching such a comely young woman model stunning clothing that she looked so good in. But even more fun was how innocent she was toward the whole thing, as if she herself couldn't believe she was wearing them. Hardly like the entitled girls he'd grown up around.

"What did you think of the dress shop? I take it you're unaccustomed to formal wear."

"For the events I did at the Toulouse office,

I wore a black suit. With my only accessory an earpiece to keep the event running."

"At the APCF function we'll have someone else wear the earpiece. You should mingle and impress the guests. You know, you look stunning in those evening gowns."

She looked down to the sand, obviously a little embarrassed by his compliment. Which, of course, made her all the cuter.

"You've gone to a lot of trouble for me already."

He winked. "I'm sure my investment will pay off."

"Hey, are princes allowed to wink?"

"I'll check the handbook. Probably not."

Zander's phone chimed in his pocket. It was a personalized ringtone he couldn't ignore.

"Hello, Mother. How is Her Highness today?" He bugged his eyes at Marie. She bit her lip in response as their toes sunk farther into the sand. "Ah, yes, Cici. I remember. But I already have a companion for the season," he explained with a glance over to Marie. "Marie Paquet, the event manager at the APCF. She's going to accompany me so that we can compare what's going on this spring with our gala plans... No, Mother, we're not dating..."

No, Mother, I don't know anything about her family... Yes, I know the press broadcasts every move we make.

He didn't respond aloud to that part of the conversation.

Signature Princess Claudine. A commoner who was fortunate enough to catch the eye of his father, His Serene Highness Prince Hugh, now ruler of Charlegin, Claudine was extremely concerned with the status and station of everyone she encountered. The princess was a master snoop.

"Thank you once again for the offer, Mother. I'll be sure to leave Abella at the palace if I feel the need to be the *dazzling young prince all the best girls want to get close to.*"

It was his sister Elise's expressed wish that she did not want Abella raised by her grandmother at the palace should anything happen to her and her husband. While Claudine was outwardly hurt that Elise had left instructions for Abella to be left in Zander's care if needed, it was clear that she was relieved not to have a baby to deal with. Generally, Her Highness was so busy with her art trips to Bali or on ski slopes in the States, she wasn't in one place for long.

More important, Elise and Valentin had

hoped to raise a child who cared about humanity as a whole, about those less fortunate and about ways to make the planet a better place. The tutelage of Claudine was not going to bestow that onto Abella.

It was Prince Hugh who had taught those values to his children. With all of Hugh's duties now that his own father had passed and the crown had come to sit on his head, Elise wasn't certain that he'd have time to spend with Abella and undo any superficial attitudes of Claudine's that might creep in. Elise wanted Zander to care for her child instead.

"Yes, Mother, the Hungarians, I'll be there." He eventually returned the phone to his pocket and turned to Marie. "My mother makes my love life her business."

"You're lucky to have someone who cares."

He wondered who cared about Marie.

"I am, but my mother and I seem to have different ideas about the matter."

"How so?"

Zander would publicly defend his family until the end of the earth, so he chose his words precisely. "She's been known to fix me up, and always with the wrong women. Now that I have Abella's necessities to consider, it's more important than ever to be careful who I have around."

"Did something happen?"

Henriette Fontaine, one of this mother's matches. That's what happened.

"I was seeing someone a few months ago who proved to not be as she appeared."

"In what way?"

Zander well understood that his family, and his subjects, expected him to marry an appropriate woman befitting a prince. While royalty might be permitted to marry commoners, his mother had always stressed to him that she should be one of the *best girls*, as she'd just repeated to him on the phone. Which had invariably led to superficial socialites who didn't see Zander as his own person, but only as a bank account and a palace.

Zander was putting dating aside completely for the time being.

"You can guess," he answered Marie. "She pretended to fall in love with Abella because she thought that was a route to my heart. I fell for her song and dance at first."

"Then what?"

"She started spending obscene amounts of my money, telling me it was on things for the baby. My accountants alerted me that instead she was buying jewelry for herself and treating her friends to lavish evenings out."

"She outright lied to you?"

"Then I started noticing that whenever I left the room, she'd completely ignore Abella even if she was crying or communicating a need."

"So she was just pretending to care about her?"

"The pièce de résistance was when she didn't realize I was standing behind her as she told her girlfriends she couldn't wait for Abella to be old enough to squire her away to boarding school."

"Wow."

"Yeah, wow," he minced and looked out to the sea. "I know I had been naive to let her near, but I was sincerely hurt by her deception."

"Of course you were."

He looked from the water to Marie's face, then quickly back again. He was surprised at how good it felt to talk to her. Words came easily.

"As you can imagine, I was totally unprepared to care for Abella when my sister and brother-in-law died. Even though Elise had made provisions in the case of her and Valentin's death, none of us expected it to actually happen."

"They were so young."

"Elise was a good and noble woman. The crown would have fit well on her head." He counted out five waves as they broke softly on the shore before retreating with the ebb of the tide. "It will be the great challenge of my life to properly raise her daughter."

At the shoreline, Marie was first to walk into the water and get her feet wet, encouraging Zander to follow. The setting sun provided a dramatic orange backdrop as they kicked their feet in the shallow tide.

It couldn't be more surprising but being with Marie, he found himself imagining an alternative to the Henriettes of the world. Having a connection with someone that was real, where two people could show each other who they truly were. Where what was inside them was what mattered. Who they could bare their souls with. Beyond crowns and titles, beyond class and wealth and facades.

Curiosity pecked at him. Claudine's earlier questioning motivated him to ask, "I'm learning that it's essential to be sensitive when asking questions about orphaned children. Do you mind my asking, how did your parents die?"

"They were killed," Marie answered dully.

Someday he'd be parlaying those same words to Abella, when she was old enough to understand them. He realized how difficult that was going to be. "That's terrible."

Marie pursed her lips, which made Zander question if either it was too painful for her to talk about it or if she didn't regard the death of her parents as terrible.

"I was eleven," she added.

His gut thudded for her.

"What a tragedy. You had no other family who could take you in?" He thought of his own situation. Although it was unusual and unnecessary for royalty to leave any sort of last will and testament, his sister, Elise, had gone to great lengths to document her daughter's care.

Marie kicked her feet in the water as she muttered, "My parents didn't have any contact with anyone else in our family so I didn't know them."

"No grandparents, no aunts or uncles?"

"They didn't speak to my parents."

"So if you weren't sent to live with relatives, what did happen?"

"Foster care. Six different placements."

"Six? Why?"

Marie's feet splashed in the water again, as if she was trying to bat away something.

"People fall in love with babies, not the older kids. Plus we don't fit into the clothes the foster parents keep around. We need things like books and phones. We eat more. The profit margin isn't as high."

"Isn't all of that controlled by the government? The foster parents get an allowance for your care."

"It's supposed to be. They try. But the system is overcrowded."

He had to resist the impulse to put his arm around her or hold her hand. He wanted to comfort her. "Did you feel love and affection from any of your foster parents?"

"Some of them were kinder than others. But it was a business to all of them." She bit her lip. "Hey, do you want to run?"

"Run?"

"Yes, right now. Let's just run."

He shrugged his shoulders. "Why not?"

And so they did. Two adults, one a prince, both in street clothes, ran along the shallow tide under the Cannes sunset.

They ran as if they were being chased.

Could they outrun their pasts, their destinies?

After they'd gone as far as they could, stopping with breath heavy from the exertion, Zander said, "I have to get back to the apartment. Iris has been with the baby all day and needs the evening. Let's order in some food and get work done for the gala."

He thought of the powerful film executives he'd agreed to have drinks with tonight and decided he'd tell them that something came up. He couldn't help but view his calendar through a different lens than he had in the past. Before Elise died. And he knew it was crazy, but being with Marie made him really acknowledge how much he'd changed. And had him appreciating Abella and the new life he'd created even more.

Once they returned from their exhilarating run on the beach, the club attendant handed them the personal items he'd locked up for them. "Your Highness."

Reading the young man's name tag, he replied, "Thank you, Stefan. Please, call me Zander."

Marie noticed that the prince spent a lot of time getting people to call him by his first name. He'd told her that outside of official occasions he absolutely hated being called by his title. He wanted to be regarded, and referred to, as a man like any other.

To be liked, judged or hated for himself, not his standing. While that did break with royal protocol, he didn't seem to care. This was a prince who rolled up his pants and ran on the beach. Who canceled his plans with

Hollywood bigwigs because he wanted to get home to his baby niece.

A lot had become clear about Zander. Marie's internet research had identified the woman he was dating a few months ago and Zander's description of her today explained why Marie hadn't seen any recent photos of them together. It probably also explained why he was so defensive yesterday, when she had picked up Abella's sippy cup and he grabbed it out of her hand. He didn't like anyone to care for the baby. Certainly not someone who'd yet to prove herself trustworthy. Not someone who, for example, was the daughter of murdered criminals.

His Highness could buy Marie all the fancy gowns in the world. But obviously she wouldn't be a real date of the prince. She'd never belong in his world. As a matter of fact, a spark of alarm came over her at the thought that being seen in public with Zander might lead to scrutiny, to someone investigating her background. Didn't the media seem to have special powers to uncover even the most obscure buried secrets? Zander would be furious if he found out she was concealing such repugnant information about herself.

Oh, how she wished her yesteryears could be erased. That they wouldn't follow her around like a shadow that decided when and for how long she'd be allowed any sunlight. The past was that gigantic lead ball she was chained to.

She'd never be free of it.

CHAPTER FIVE

"Is THIS SIMILAR to the corporate events you've been working on?" Zander joked with Marie as they were welcomed to the Laublie Foundation for Breast Cancer Research's "A Night in Mexico." After passing through the photographers and security to get into the private party space, guests found themselves in an interior courtyard rimmed by one-story white stucco buildings with red roofs.

An enormous stone fountain dominated the center of the area. Water burst from the center of it in a high and wide spray, accentuated by colored lights alternating between milky white, bright red and sharp green denoting the colors of the Mexican flag.

"Just a little different than my typical sandwich luncheon," Marie chuckled.

The courtyard was packed with party attendees as still more made their way in.

"And you weren't kidding about guests taking the theme and dress code seriously."

"It's fun, isn't it? Don't you feel different in your gown, senorita?"

Of course she did. She'd never worn anything even close to the finery of the black lace gown with the colorful floral embroidery Zander had bought her a few days ago. But the people here probably wore luxe clothing every day, like he did.

So this was grown-up dress up, Marie thought. Surely a rich man's pleasure.

As an adolescent, moving from foster home to foster home with a tattered suitcase holding her only belongings, Marie had one itchy and pilled long black dress that she'd wear if she needed to be formal.

She remembered one time as a teenager when the school planned a dance. The girls in her class talked for weeks about shopping for new outfits and showed up in pretty party dresses. All Marie had was the ratty black dress.

The other students rolled their eyes as if that was exactly what they expected of her. As much as teenagers often complained about their parents, their troubles were nothing compared with the sloppy girl who didn't have a family at all.

Those nasty kids had no idea what it was like to be left an orphan at eleven years old. No one wanted a preteen like her. Babies stood a chance of being chosen for adoption. She was just a paycheck for her foster parents. Shuffled around, with no one taking an interest in her. Nowhere she ever thought of as home.

"You look incredible," Zander said, bringing her back to the courtyard, "if I neglected to mention it before."

He had sent a hair and makeup artist to style Marie for the evening. Her hair was coiffed into a dramatic sideswipe that curled into a low bun at the side of her neck. Behind her ear was a cluster of fresh red and yellow flowers, which had been delivered to her by courier earlier today.

The flower arrival had set her heart aflame. It was easy enough to fantasize that chivalrous Prince Zander was her date and that he'd sent flowers with a romantic note professing how much he was looking forward to their evening, or some such sentiment.

When she opened the box to see that it was the hairpiece she was to give the stylist employed to get her ready, Marie was a little disappointed. But, of course, this wasn't a date so there was no reason for flowers. Although the fragrant blooms arrived in a gold box tied with a ribbon, she knew it was of no more importance to Zander than if it had been a box of paper files.

Nonetheless, the whole outfit came together beautifully. And since they'd yet to speak to anyone, the fact that she wasn't a society doyenne on the arm of the prince hadn't been uncovered.

"Would you like a drink?" Zander didn't wait for an answer as he took two from the tray a waiter presented. Frosty margaritas in heavy blue glasses were prepared traditionally with salt along the rim.

Coming toward Marie and Zander were two flashy women. One a blonde with her hair up in a snug bun and wearing a pastel green dress that was so tight Marie could count the woman's ribs. She was with a redhead whose long curls were spiraled into a bun that looked of the breakfast pastry variety.

"Zander!" one called out.

"Your Highness!" the other echoed.

"Yikes," Zander whispered into Marie's ear, the warmth from his breath making her neck bend involuntarily in his direction. "I know those two. Quickly, to the tortillas." He gestured toward the other side of the courtyard where cooks in traditional Mexican garb were pressing balls of dough onto the blistering-hot *comal* grill.

Zander and Marie crept in that direction, the prince keeping watch as the two women caught sight of what they were doing. Marie could tell that he felt like game in the wild being chased by predators. One couldn't blame those girls, though, for being interested in Zander. Although he claimed that he was always surrounded by women who were only after the lifestyle and luxury that his title brought, he might have been missing one key component.

His Highness Zander de Nellay of Charlegin was one crazy-hot prince. Full stop. Indisputable. No doubt about it. And especially tonight, so dapper in his Mexican-style tuxedo with its stitching on the lapels, perfectly fitted to his tall and muscular frame. No wonder women lunged at him with hunting nets.

In fact, Marie still couldn't quite believe this remarkable man was her date, even if it was only for educational purposes.

"Oh, no, you don't," the blonde shrieked as she caught up with Zander and Marie, her redheaded cohort tagging along. "You owe me a dance back from the concert on Mykonos last summer."

"We haven't seen much of you this year, Zander. We heard you aren't dating Henriette anymore." The redhead trailed on the blonde's heels. "Have we lost you to that adorable baby daughter of yours?"

"Niece," he piped quickly.

"I'm fabulous with babies! You should let me help you take care of her," the blonde said as the heel of her white-, red-and green-sequined stiletto got caught between two of the stone tiles in the courtyard, causing her to lurch forward. A grimace twisted her face.

"I love babies, too." The redhead was not to be outdone. "They're so squishy and roly."

"I don't know that humans were intended for squishing and rolling but I appreciate your inquiry," Zander clipped in a tight baritone. "Ladies, if you'll excuse us, I see someone I've got to talk to."

Behind them, the blonde called out, "But Zander, you haven't introduced us to your date!"

Zander said to Marie as he pulled her away, "I think I told you, being a *royal bachelor* has its challenges."

"You have to always remain polite. That must be hard."

"Protocol demands that I conduct myself appropriately. I always seem to attract the prince groupies who make that a battle. Who don't want to really know me at all. They just want to be part of my advantaged life. Which is a far cry from forming genuine relationships."

"Judging books by their covers, as the saying goes." Marie knew all about that. She was constantly being evaluated against her troubled childhood. Just as she was sure Zander would judge her if he knew who her parents really were.

"I do the tuxedoes and the yachts but, day to day, I align myself with these charities so that I can help them get on with the work of improving lives."

"Your face is a double-edged sword, then."

A wistful smile came across Zander's face.

"With Abella in my care, I wish I could keep all these hangers-on away."

"Let's go inside," she offered, almost as a comfort.

Inside the ballroom, traditional dancers performed while shaking percussive maracas. Their full skirts created waves of color as they swayed through their steps and enchanted the guests.

"Marie, are you taking in all of the specifics?" Zander concerned himself with the matter at hand. "This is wonderful event design, with the margaritas and the *comal* out in the courtyard as an entry to the party."

"Yes, it was a total transition from the outside world into the private space of the party. Look at those." She pointed to the ceiling, where dozens of piñatas in the shapes of animals were hung at various lengths. "It's just gorgeous."

"Like you," he said and leaned down to give her a tiny kiss on the cheek.

Marie froze in place, stunned.

Her eyes pierced into his and her heart thumped against her chest.

After listening to it beat countless times, she snapped out of her hold. "Would you excuse me for a moment? I'm going to find the ladies' room."

Zander hadn't meant to kiss Marie. Hadn't meant to at all!

Why had he, why had he? His brain throbbed, and would until it had its answer. Maybe it was after being approached by those two aggressive party girls. Who reminded him of Henriette and the endless parade of awful women who had defined his life thus far. Marie was so definitely not like any of them. And he found himself opening up to her, perhaps actually too much.

But, in any case, a kiss on the cheek was merely a sociable gesture, right? He hoped that was it, although he wouldn't swear to that conclusion.

Unfortunately, his mouth wouldn't stop vibrating after the feel of his lips against Marie's cheek. Surely the clouds in the sky weren't as soft as her delicate skin. His mouth had barely brushed across her face but his body reacted as if a firecracker had exploded inside him.

His behavior was dangerous. It was shocking how he hadn't had any control of himself in the moment after he'd confided in her about the royal gold diggers. His mouth was propelled to Marie's face as if an outside power had deemed it and there was nothing he could do but obey the command.

Everyone pecked everyone on the cheek at events like this, he reasoned with himself. It was no big deal. Marie had probably forgotten about a minute after it happened. He would, too.

As those reassurances ticked across his mind, he knew they were lies. The kiss dilated his eyes with desire, both physical and emotional. It was as if he hadn't known how hungry he was until someone handed him a crust of bread. He suddenly felt as if he was starving.

However, this was no time in his life to sate that craving.

He could surely have physical contact with a woman if he wanted to. After the APCF gala. And with a female other than Marie. He was free to have dalliances that meant nothing to him, and not under the same roof as Abella, of course. But there'd be no getting serious with anyone for many years to come, if ever.

Indeed, after Henriette, it had been dawning on him more and more that if he were ever to marry, his wife would effectively become Abella's mother. Not only would he have to find someone he could trust with his niece's safety and well-being, whoever he was with would have to be able and willing to accept Abella as part of the package. To be a good influence on her and to genuinely love her like her own. Zander would accept nothing less. It was a tall order.

Frankly, he doubted he'd ever meet someone like that. Which was fine with him. Abella was the one in line for the throne. As Zander was Elise's younger brother, he was not obliged to produce heirs. If he never married it might appear unconventional but wouldn't harm the royal family in any way.

So why was it that everything about Marie

had thrown him into a brainstorm of new ideas and new contradictions?

Prince Zander never took his eyes off Marie as she crossed the ballroom to rejoin him after finding the ladies' room. The look on his face was off. Nostrils flared, his eyes appeared darker and darker as she approached until, at short distance, they looked almost angry. After a mental adjustment she was able to perceive, he softened but only a little.

"I was wondering why you were gone so long," he said as he presented his arm for her to slip hers through. At the feel of her hand against his muscles, sparks prickled her.

She knew she had spent a lot of time away from him after she'd excused herself, but she'd needed time to recover. In a tiny garden area that was not part of the event space, she'd practiced the deep-breathing techniques that had gotten her through many difficult situations. Of course, she'd never had to call upon them because she'd just been kissed by an unbelievably sexy prince!

Bringing her hand to the exact spot where his lips made contact with her cheek, she'd looked up to the moon and asked it for composure. Obviously, Zander had meant the peck in a context where everyone kissed each other on the cheek as a simple pleasantry. He wasn't attracted to her or any such nonsense. He'd never know that he made her knees go as weak as if she'd drunk one of those margaritas that she actually dared not touch.

She hoped she appeared calm when, really, her legs were still wobbly.

"Take note of all of the little touches here," Zander instructed her as they recommitted to exploring the party. Of course, the kiss a few minutes ago was long gone from his mind. Proof of its irrelevance. He was professional, and she'd be the same. Outwardly, at least.

The ballroom was, indeed, decorated to the hilt in red, green and white. Massive displays of flowers sat on every table atop vividly colored tablecloths.

"These settings are outstanding," she said of the table arrangements utilizing traditional Mexican pottery rather than fancy china. "Those kinds of choices make a huge difference."

"Exactly."

"A gala of this scale must cost a fortune to produce. Doesn't that cut down the proceeds from the event?"

"There's an old expression. *It takes money to make money.* And an organization this prominent does get a lot of the components donated. The APCF isn't as high profile as the Laublie Foundation. But we can stake our place on the scene."

"That's why you want this year's gala to be spectacular."

"Right. So that next year I can ask for sponsors and underwriting, and point to our annual fund-raiser as one of the best events of the Cannes social season."

"Building a reputation."

"Even if I have to spend a lot of my own money on the gala this year, I'm taking the long view of how it might pay off in years to come."

"Did you support the APCF before you started taking care of Abella?" Marie remained so buzzy from his kiss she hoped she wasn't babbling.

Zander still seemed skewed, too. He was such a polite man, he was likely worried that she'd misinterpret the little kiss he'd given her. That she'd take license to believe it had significance when, in fact, it didn't. Plus, he'd probably surprised even himself when he shared some feelings with her about the people in his life. Funny that Marie was doing a better job at keeping secrets than he was.

The lights began to flash red to green

to white to indicate that it was time for the guests to take their seats. As Zander led Marie to their table, she wasn't surprised that theirs was up front and center to the stage.

The first course of the meal was served, sweet yellow corn tamales.

As they began eating, other guests at the table kept a vigilant eye on the prince's companion. Would she choose the wrong fork or some other social faux pas that would broadcast her lack of pedigree?

Although their tablemates weren't titled, Marie guessed that none of them was the daughter or son of criminals who were murdered during a drug deal. That their parents didn't leave them in an empty apartment where they were alone and hungry for three days until a neighbor noticed something was amiss and called the police. Nor was it likely that they were tossed to and from foster homes where they were treated with a spectrum that ranged only from tolerance to neglect.

As Marie spiraled, she was about to excuse herself again to find a quiet place to do her breathing exercises. But Zander sensed that she was distraught and asked the waiter to bring her a glass of ice water. "You all right?"

Sipping slowly, she nodded and was able to regain her composure.

With colorful beams shooting in every direction, a trumpet heralded from the back of the ballroom. In came a twelve-man mariachi band, brandishing horns and guitars and violins as they began to play. In costumes of fitted pants with silver buttons down the outer leg, matching jackets and traditional wide-brimmed sombrero hats, the musicians marched into the ballroom in two lines, bringing with them a wall of sound so thrilling and effervescent it made Marie's spirit soar.

After their dramatic entrance, the band members then dispersed throughout the room while they played, stopping at different tables to perform little solos or to flirt with the older ladies and add additional good cheer. The ballroom palpitated with energy. Marie fully understood what an unforgettable event this was.

The mariachis entertained during the entrée of fish Veracruz, then speeches were made and the fund-raising auction brought in lots of money. Several people came over to the table to pay their respects to, or flirt with, the prince. And Zander introduced Marie as his colleague at the APCF, encouraging them to attend their upcoming gala, as well.

Once the crowd thinned, Zander stood and

pulled out Marie's chair for her to join him. "Let's go outside."

Back out at the courtyard, clusters of people stood conversing in the night air. Some watched a Mexican sandal-making demonstration. Zander brought Marie to a quieter corner where a lone musician sat on a brick ledge strumming a very large and unusual guitar. The melody was sweet and sad. Marie found herself completely mesmerized as each note wafted up into the dark sky toward the bright moon.

The moment was profoundly romantic. Zander seemed to take notice of Marie's enjoyment and put his arm around her shoulder. Together they watched the face of the guitarist as he plucked emotion out of each note, conveying more than lyrics ever could.

Zander's arm around Marie all but made her woozy. Not knowing whether she should or not, her head decided for her and fell backward onto his shoulder. He instinctively pulled her closer. In that prolonged interlude, a moment frozen in time, she allowed herself to dream about things she'd never dared before.

About what it would be like to walk through life with someone. Not a someone like her ex Gerard who thought he was too good for her. But someone who was secure, who knew that by lifting up his partner together they could reach untold highs. That was how Zander made her feel. No one in the world had ever made her feel anything even close to that before.

Indisputable facts quickly worked to pull her down from the heaven she was ascending to. Zander was never going to be with a woman like her, with a squalid past that would hang over them like a cloud for the rest of their lives. Imagine if the media found out who she was and looked into her background to see whom Prince Zander de Nellay of Charlegin was traipsing around Cannes with!

And even if that wasn't an issue, he had Abella as his priority. Uncle Prince Zander was clearly not ready to let a woman have a permanent place in his life and wouldn't be for a long time yet, something he'd articulated very clearly. Marie respected him for that. It was actually something she greatly admired about him. No one in Marie's life had ever looked out for her as he was for his niece.

It was no surprise that baby Abella had Zander's heart. Earlier this week, after they had gone shopping for the gowns and then ran on the beach, they'd gone back to his apartment to work. As soon as the nanny brought the baby into the room, Zander's eyes lit up. He held her as a father would, firmly in one arm, close and secure. Not like an inexperienced bachelor who'd had a baby foisted upon him. He was natural and authentic with Abella, as if her care came organically to him.

Zander had ordered pasta from the café next door and dutifully cut up small pieces for Abella as he and Marie ate. She'd had experience with babies as the foster homes she'd lived in housed multiple ages of children and she'd been expected to help with the younger kids. So when Zander got a phone call, it was quite logical that Marie could hold Abella.

Instead, Zander paced the opulent living room while he took his call, lifting the baby in one arm and talking through an earpiece. While part of Marie was a little offended that he wouldn't let her hold Abella, she honored his distrust, especially after that disloyal Henriette he had told her about. Marie knew he'd only even allowed her into his apartment because they had so much to do for the gala and her being an employee of the APCF lent her some credibility.

When Marie got back to her room that night, she allowed herself a few minutes of musings on Zander and Abella.

About the loving family they made together. About almond-eyed children of her own.

Then she forced herself to shut those thoughts down because dreams never did her any good.

Just like the moment at hand, with the romantic Mexican guitar, the brilliant moon and Zander's arm around her.

In fact, as soon as Zander realized he'd had his arm around her shoulder for a while, he withdrew it. Leaving her as cold as if she was left naked in a blizzard.

They both knew nothing amorous was ever going to develop between them, and he must have reminded himself that people were watching.

Every fiber in her being screamed in protest when he withdrew his arm. Her soul cried out for him to instead take her into a full embrace. To kiss her not just again on the cheek but on her lips, her neck and even more intimate spots on her body.

That was never to be. She was going to parade around Cannes with a dynamic and gracious prince. But that would be that.

Not only would there be no romance with Zander, there couldn't even be hot reckless nights where she'd satisfy her physical attraction to him and then be done with it. The prince's casual-affair days were over. Just as well because, if she was being honest, Marie didn't think she could handle a fling with him that would come to an abrupt end.

Although she knew that she'd spend the rest of her life remembering his one and only kiss on the cheek and his one strong arm around her.

But Marie and Zander were in a business relationship. One she was fortunate to have.

Any other thoughts were just pure self-torture.

CHAPTER SIX

FUNKY MUSIC KEPT Zander company as he
dressed for the film festival party at the
Carlsmon Hotel. He'd fueled through a busy
afternoon and now he wanted upbeat sounds
to pump him up for the evening. He pulled on
the pants of his tuxedo and removed the coordinating shirt from its hanger in his closet.
Catching his image in the full-length mirror,
he engaged in a staredown with his own face.

The unsettled feeling that beat through him
was not coming from the rhythms of the song
he was listening to. No, the shake-up had one
basis and one basis alone. Marie Paquet. Despite everything he had been telling himself
about not becoming attached to anyone, she
had gotten under his skin. As a matter of fact,
thoughts of her were all but driving him mad.

Buttoning up the shirt and tucking it into
his pants, he asked his reflection some questions. First and foremost, how did he allow

himself to plant that kiss on her cheek at the Mexico party when he'd intended nothing of the sort?

Fastening his cuff links, he commanded his eyes in the mirror to tell him why later, when the evening was winding down and they were listening to the gentle guitar in the courtyard, he put his arm around her shoulder in a way that coworkers would not have touched each other?

The Zander in the mirror had no right answers, which was an unusual predicament for him to be in. He was usually the man with all the solutions. Marie had thrown him off balance and he was losing his footing.

"You must stop this now," he reprimanded aloud to his own reflection.

But as he threaded on his tie and straightened it under the collar of his shirt, a voice inside him told him otherwise.

Marie was a breath of fresh air. Because she was so unaccustomed to the lifestyle he led, she didn't covet it. She was utterly guileless, and he never got the sense she wanted something from him, other than his help with the APCF gala. And that allowed him to tap into himself in a way that felt so pure, so emancipating.

Sitting on the bed to put on his socks and

shoes, vitality coursed through him when he replayed over and over again that seemingly innocent kiss he'd given Marie. It wasn't harmless at all if he took into account the fact that he hadn't been able to stop thinking of it since. And it wasn't just one brush on the cheek that he couldn't get his brain to move past. No, it was the accompanying thoughts he was having about caressing and kissing every inch of her.

A voice low inside him demanded more. More touch, more whispers and personal conversations and knowing nods that made him believe he had some kind of special bond with her.

At his core, he knew that human connections were illogical. Attraction didn't know or care if two people were so socially separated that they would be expected to have nothing in common. Desire hadn't an inkling that one person was fed with a silver spoon while the other might not have had enough to eat. Fates weren't the slightest bit interested in how something looked to the masses. Destiny knew only the truth it saw before itself.

As he slid one arm and then the other through the sleeves of his tuxedo jacket, Zander finished dressing and begged himself to stop thinking about Marie. She'd be accompanying him tonight and to a few more events. They'd do the APCF benefit and then have no reason to spend time together. If the fund-raiser was a hit, perhaps Marie would get the permanent job in Cannes and he'd see her once a year if he continued to chair the gala. Other than that, there would be no cause for their worlds to collide after this season.

The babbling he heard from Abella's baby monitor fortified Zander's priority. This precious baby was what mattered, and everything else took second place. Besides, he'd only just gotten acquainted with Marie. One side of his brain questioned the wisdom of even having her in the apartment. Though he'd bet his life that she wasn't out to deceive him in any way, some people were masters at concealing things.

Were he ever to decide to be with a woman he'd need to spend months, if not years, vetting her before he'd begin to trust her around Abella, which his mistake with Henriette reinforced.

After grabbing his phone and wallet, he slipped into Abella's room. Iris had the crown princess in her lap on the rocking chair.

"Are you okay for the evening?" he asked the nanny.

"Thank you, yes. Have a good time."

Zander couldn't resist tiptoeing over to give Abella a little kiss on the top of her head. As he stepped out of the room she clucked, "Bye, Da."

In front of the building where Marie was staying, Zander had his driver park so that he could greet her as she came out of the lobby. The pewter-colored gown with the geometric cutouts looked even more stunning and sexy on her than he had remembered when they bought it together.

"You are absolutely breathtaking," he couldn't help commenting as she walked toward him.

"Thank you for sending the hair and makeup squad again," she demurred with a modest smile. "I feel very glamorous." Her locks had doubled in volume and some kind of tiny shimmers were magically affixed to various strands, highlighting her expertly made-up face.

"You'd better, since the Hollywood A-list is going to be at this party."

"Just another ordinary evening for me," she joked, the sweetest blush coming to her cheeks.

Zander's chest swelled with a particular pride as he helped Marie, and the formidable train of her evening gown, into the car.

He hoped he'd done enough to make sure she felt put together, knowing that meeting movie stars wasn't exactly something she was used to.

When they arrived at the Carlsmon, Zander repeated his ministrations to help Marie and the dress through the car door.

Over a hundred years old, the Carlsmon Hotel was a masterful example of French Art Nouveau architecture. It had always been one of the key meeting places for the film festival set. Countless movies and music videos had been filmed there. An enormous structure, its two distinctive domes on both the seaward corners were rumored to be inspired in design by the breasts of the architect's wife. It was, without question, the most recognizable building in Cannes.

Hundreds of cameras greeted Zander and Marie with blinding flashes. He had figured that a prince of a tiny principality was not so interesting at an event where award-winning actors and actresses would be in attendance.

Nonetheless, there was always a hungry market for photos of young royals doing anything at all. He didn't know if his appearance at this party would warrant enough attention that the press would recognize Marie as the woman he was with at the Mexico party. She wasn't used to having her name in the papers and gossip sites, so he hoped they could just pass under the radar on a night filled with brighter stars.

He gestured to take Marie's arm, which was becoming a much too familiar habit. His shoulders arched on their own volition when she gripped his bicep as they made their way down the red carpet to enter the hotel.

Behind barricades, members of the general public were allowed to congregate and take photos, calling out to the stars who waved and posed.

Marie's eyes went wide at the sight of some very recognizable faces.

Incoming party guests were ushered into the event space, a ballroom that had been converted into a screening room for the night. Ten or so movie screens were erected around the room with comfortable seating arrangements set up in clusters in front of each. With about three hundred in attendance, guests would enjoy finger foods and cocktails while they watched a documentary produced by two notable actresses on the issues of illiteracy. Proceeds from the evening were to benefit an international education organization.

"Zander!"

He recognized the voice of Asher Kraus,

the Austrian race car driver he'd known for years. In years gone by, Zander and Asher had been known to rent a ski chalet where they entertained the party people of Europe for winter getaways. A time in Zander's life that seemed so shallow now.

Zander let go of Marie, noting the disquieting change to his body chemistry without her touch, in order to give his old pal a proper hug.

"This is my colleague, Marie Paquet."

"Colleague?" Asher raised an eyebrow, as if Zander had been using that word as a metaphor for something else.

As a matter of fact, he'd been making a point of introducing Marie as a colleague to as many people as possible to help her build a reputation as a relevant fund-raiser. Plus, he didn't want anyone to have a cheapened image of her, to assume she was merely eye candy on the bachelor prince's arm.

Nobody would understand the turmoil that rollicked through Zander as he referred to her as a professional contact.

"Sit with us," Asher interrupted Zander's contemplations as he guided the prince and Marie over to the group he was sitting with. A stylish bunch, to be sure. Bendy women held wineglasses while the urbane men argued about which country produced the best cabernets.

The lights dimmed for the screening. Zander and Marie sat next to each other on a small sofa. Her gown's halter top and cutouts left quite a lot of her skin uncovered and, before even meaning to, Zander made one long slide with his hand down her back as a way of ensuring she was comfortable.

The motion left him anything but, as the silken feel of her shot a maddening craving to his very center. After flashing on the number of things he'd like to explore with her while in the dark of a movie screening, he straightened up and vowed to keep his hands to himself.

One of the film's producers took to the central podium to introduce the screening.

"I love how they've done the food." Marie gestured to the cocktail tables in front of them, which adorned every grouping throughout the room. Movie theater food had been elevated to a Carlsmon Hotel level of posh. Old-timey red-and-white boxes held four different flavors of popcorn. Hot buttered, spicy, chocolate caramel and cheddar cheese all looked tempting.

"Let's try these." Zander popped one kernel into Marie's mouth and another into his own. He figured she wouldn't want to risk getting any popcorn dust on her dress. Or he wanted an excuse to feed her. He acknowledged both possibilities. Careful not to let his fingers touch her lips in the process, he fed them one of each flavor. As if they were merely conducting an inspection. Which they were.

And which shouldn't have bordered on the erotic.

Even though it did.

"That chocolate caramel is to die for," she voted in.

Bottles of old-fashioned sodas were kept cold in ice buckets. Trays with several types of sausages inside brioche rolls were the evening's equivalent of American hot dogs.

Small plastic bags lay on a tray next to bowls of assorted candies. Guests were invited to fill the bags to their liking so that they could nibble during the movie.

"Would you like me to make you a bag?" Zander asked. Asher and his friends made their selections, as well.

"I can do it," Marie insisted, helping herself to a box of the popcorn, an orange soda and a mix of every candy offered. So much for concern about her dress. Zander grinned with satisfaction. He liked a girl who chose candy over worrying about her designer gown.

Admittedly, he found himself wanting to watch her more than he did the film, but he put his attention to the screening once it began. It was quite effective in its discussion about the literacy issue and its impact on education, identity and employment.

Once the screening was over, the Carlsmon staff worked like rapid fire to remove the movie-watching groupings and turn the space back to a ballroom so that dancing and coffee service could begin.

"Let's go look at the auction items."

"Yes, I'd like to see them."

Zander took Marie's hand, oh, so supple, to navigate them over to the silent auction area.

"Yowza!" he exclaimed when they reached one of the display tables. "These are going to bring in serious money. That yellow gold and diamond watch could fetch a quarter of a million on its own."

Marie read aloud the description that accompanied a photo collage of a tropical retreat. "Weeklong stay on a private island in the South Pacific. You and eleven guests, plus a full staff, will be the only inhabitants on this hundred-acre island. Small boats and everything else you'll need to indulge in water sports and leisure pursuits will be provided. Your fun in the sun will be rewarded with meals prepared by a Michelin-starred chef. This unique property has eight bedrooms and ten bathrooms. Bidding begins at five hundred thousand."

"Nice package."

"You people live in an entirely parallel universe to the rest of us."

"You people?" he laughed.

"Let's not pretend I know what a 1963 B-Series convertible is."

Zander read the description. "Considered the best in class, this classic design has been fully updated with electronic ignition, modern sound system, wireless navigation and top-speed capability. The interior's luxury will be the envy of every motorist on the road. Bidding begins at nine hundred thousand."

Marie bugged out her eyes. "And all of these auction items were donated?"

"The gauntlet has been thrown down to us for the APCF gala, Mademoiselle Paquet. Let's see what we can do."

She filled her cheeks with air like balloons about to pop.

The band started up with a slow song, a baritone voice belting out endearments of love. People took to the dance floor.

"May I have this dance?"

* * *

As the prince led Marie to the dance floor, she was immediately swept into the music. The five-piece band was fronted by a charismatic crooner who sang about love being there all along if someone was looking for it.

When Zander circled his arm around Marie's waist for the slow dance, hearing the word *love* being sung at the same time made her light-headed. It wasn't a word she'd heard a lot in her life.

With his hand flat against her back, Zander brought her in close to him. She stiffened to his touch at first. It was simply too pleasurable, and rather than get pulled into those hands like they were a mighty wave of the ocean she tried to bolster herself at shore. While she couldn't keep a physical distance, she knew that she had to keep an emotional one.

Taking her hand in his spare one, Zander swayed them in a one-and-two, one-and-two that was something in between ballroom dancing and a more contemporary slide. They were joined so tightly that she could only press her face into the lapel of his tux. If there was a better spot on earth, Marie surely didn't know of it.

The formal fabric of his jacket smelled of

a light musky cologne, nothing overbearing. The rock-hard muscles of his chest matched the solidly built arms she'd become quite familiar with. In fact, physical proximity to Zander was something she was starting to get used to, although she suspected it wasn't a very good idea.

In a few days' time, she'd been transformed from a dowdy nonprofit worker dressed in creased trousers to a woman immersed in the glitzy lifestyle of the Cannes social scene. Zander was right when he'd told her this was something she'd need to get comfortable with if she was going to be a force in the fund-raising world. With pride that she'd gotten off to an excellent start, one problem loomed large.

How could anyone be expected to spend night and day with His Highness Prince Zander de Nellay of Charlegin and not become romantically attracted to him? And wish for something beyond their professional connection? Especially when, so far, he'd kissed her on the cheek, put his arm around her, walked arm in arm and now danced with her.

Innocent enough encounters but, nonetheless, moments that awoke her from the inside and made her entire body respond. And birthed deliberations about belonging and permanence and a life shared.

On top of all of that, not only was the prince spectacularly good-looking, he was moral and caring and had a great sense of fun. Traits that would make him a fine father figure.

Even if Abella wasn't in the picture, Marie knew that royalty had an obligation to their subjects to marry the right people. After all, there were ceremonies to preside over, elders to appease and history to uphold. Royal marriages were still the serious and exclusive business that they had been for centuries.

In a million years, Marie Paquet would never be approved as a mate for Zander. A fact she kept repeating to herself as the influence of his hands directed her across the dance floor and his low vibrato murmured in her ear, "We certainly are spending a lot of time together."

"Felice had told me to report directly to you and to put any other work aside until the gala."

"Report directly to me," Zander hummed and started to say something, then decided against it. Had he been about to say that he liked the sound of that, having Marie at his beck and call? Part of her wished he did, as confirmation that he was enjoying being thrown together as much as she was.

Which was ridiculous thinking. Yet she couldn't help musing.

If only she could meet a man like Zander someday. One whom she could actually have and hold and cherish, of course.

Photographers circled the dance floor. Several were documenting the evening for the film producers who would be able to point to a successful launch at Cannes to bring attention to their film. But Marie suspected some of the pictures being snapped were going to entertainment magazines and gossip websites, as the public never tired of gawking at celebrities.

One woman dressed in a black T-shirt and black pants swooped down and around the dancing couples as she worked to get her shots. And who could blame her?

The auburn-haired actress who'd received critical acclaim for her performance as a Holocaust survivor was grinding raunchily up against the award-winning actor now making a fortune with his action hero franchise.

There was the middle-aged couple, a respected director and his television star wife, who had reportedly split up but had eyes for only each other tonight.

A camera's flash came toward Zander and Marie, temporarily blinding her with the power of its brightness. Marie hoped the media would have no interest in finding out whom Prince Zander was spotted with in Cannes. Although royal gossip hounds noted his every public move, clearly Marie wasn't famous. Even if they were to dig, there'd probably be little or no available information about her.

She hoped not, anyway. Prince Zander shouldn't be mixed up with the likes of someone who had a background such as hers.

When the music changed, Zander expertly twirled Marie around the dance floor while continuing their conversation. "Tomorrow we have to finalize the costume theme."

"Okay," Marie acknowledged although now her mind had wandered far, far away. To those facts she'd rather keep private. To the eleven-year-old who had to carry in her gut the information that her parents were drug dealers who were killed during street warfare.

"We have to meet with the caterer, as well. I want to design a signature cocktail for the evening."

Marie nodded but her mind was still years back, on those same parents who were addicted to drugs themselves and made one careless mistake after the other until rival dealers were easily able to trip them up.

After some focused breathing, Marie was able to return her attention to the tall, powerful, sure prince she was dancing with. "Signature cocktail? I've never heard of that."

"When you've gone to a hundred of these parties, believe me it's the little niceties that make an impression."

He'd certainly made an impression on her. This man, with his selfless commitment to his orphaned niece, would make it his business to be sure Abella was never put in dangerous situations or in harm's way. It's what decent people did for their children.

As she continued to dance with Zander, she looked around the ballroom. Well-tended people chitchatted and sipped espressos. Marie knew that money or privilege didn't guarantee happiness. Had any of them known the embarrassment she had? The loss, the loneliness? Different circumstances, but the same pain?

Zander tightened his grip on her, an action she didn't protest. No, quite the opposite. She leaned into him, his broad chest and long arms providing the shelter that she rarely had the opportunity to seek.

Just for a minute, she told herself, as she closed her eyes and let the world slip away. She pressed into Zander to let him become her talisman, her beacon in the dark seas, her good luck charm, her hope. Just for a minute.

Marie wanted to dance for a long time, with no protest from Zander. Eventually, they stepped off the dance floor to check out the desserts. He was sure something had changed within her while they were dancing, although he couldn't put his finger on what. Now, when he looked over to see if she liked the lavish chocolate fountains, one dark, one milk and one white, Marie was not focused on the sweets. She had a distant, almost scared, look on her face.

"Yes, they're lovely," she managed in a monotone voice. "It's decadent to have three different flavors."

The words came out of her mouth as if someone else was saying them. While he intended to keep discussing the dessert, he felt an almost undeniable impulse to reach over and take her face in his hands. To kiss her over and over until whatever weighed so heavily in those blue eyes could be cast aside while their lips said everything without talking.

Lately, he'd been giving thought to what was next in his life. What the permanence and obligation of raising Abella would bring him. How and where he wanted to spend his days.

Gazing at Marie's sweet face and replaying the internal agony he'd perceived in her triggered protective feelings. He was starting to wonder if the devotion he had for Abella couldn't also extend to a romantic love he might have room for someday.

He subtly pointed to a couple of older women at the fountains who were laughing and making a production of preparing their deserts. Skewers had been provided for guests to create spears of fruit chunks and small squares of cake that they then passed under the fountains to coat them in chocolate. The ladies were discovering that they could pass their creations under not one, not two, but all three flavors of the chocolate, creating a drippy mess that was probably delicious.

"That's a kind of specialty food that guests tell friends about the next day," Marie said.

"Exactly."

Zander's phone buzzed in his pocket, and while he generally made a rule of not taking calls while he was out with people, the vibrating sequence was specific to a text from Iris.

Abella is ill. I've given her medication and we're sitting up for the time being.

"What's wrong?" Marie snapped to attention having read the concern in Zander's face.

"The baby is sick. Have we observed enough here for tonight?"

"From what's written in the program, it looks like there will be more speeches coming."

"I'd like to bow out early and get home." Zander uttered a phrase he'd heard himself say a lot lately.

Nothing could have prepared him for the priority a child would take in his life. He knew that he'd climb mountains or swim oceans for Abella. Giving up the hobnobbing he'd spent much of his adult life doing was easy, and evenings like tonight had become the exception, not the norm.

"Are you going home now?" Marie's eyes became very round as she asked.

"Yes."

"Oh. Okay," she said, opening and closing her fists.

"*We* are going now," he clarified, grasping that she thought he was going to leave her at the party. Relief washed over her. He outstretched his hand for hers, not taking the pleasantness he felt when she did the same for granted. "Shall we?"

Exiting the party into the starry night, they

watched as one of the most famous actors on earth, Ross Jarrell, made a late arrival to pandemonium from the fans who were still outside the hotel hoping for a celebrity sighting. With that much-talked-about *it* factor, confidence and sheen emanated from his every pore.

He wore his tux like it was a second skin, a shiny watch peeking out from his jacket sleeve. With a complexion no doubt polished to perfection by the world's finest estheticians, if not plastic surgeons, and a hair color chosen to erase any unwanted years, his perfection made him look almost unreal. Admirers screamed his name, and he stopped to wave for them and for the media.

"Nobody does glamour like the Hollywood crowd, do they?" It was a rhetorical question requiring no answer as Zander's driver appeared at the curb and ferried them away.

In his haste to get home, Zander realized he should have had his driver drop Marie off at her room. She was not in the fold of his life and didn't need to be around Abella with her not feeling well. But Marie at his side had, strangely, become the norm and it didn't occur to him.

When they arrived at Zander's apartment, Abella was sleeping on Iris's lap.

"She seems to be feeling better," the nanny reported.

After tossing off his tuxedo jacket, he picked up the baby. "Thank you so much, Iris. My driver is downstairs waiting to take you home."

With Abella in the crook of his left shoulder as had become a familiar position for both of them, he walked around the living room knowing she was always reassured by the bit of motion. Her breathing sounded a bit congested but she didn't feel feverish, to his relief.

He looked over to his companion in her gorgeous gown. She was now having to move toys out of the way so she could sit down. "Marie, if you'd like, my driver can take you home, as well." More relaxed to see that the baby probably had little more than a head cold, he added, "Or I'm going to sit up with Abella for a while, so if you're not exhausted, we could get a little work done."

As if he'd asked a question of international importance, he eagerly awaited her answer. Given his druthers, he most definitely hoped she'd stay rather than leave right away.

"Sure, I have an idea I want to talk to you about."

Iris collected her things and headed to the door. "If there's nothing else you need…"

"Marie, would you like to get out of that dress? Iris, do you have something comfortable she can borrow?"

"Second shelf in the hallway cabinet. Help yourself."

"Thank you," Marie said to the older woman. "Good night."

"Good night."

After Iris stepped out, Zander reached under the sleeping baby to undo his tie.

"What was the idea you were talking about?"

"It was when we were leaving the Carlsmon and we saw Ross Jarrell arrive. I was thinking how much he looked like a movie star from another era."

He heartily agreed, as Jarrell had captured Zander's attention in that moment, too. Though he'd met Ross at other events, seeing him on the red carpet with the massive fanfare and the hundreds of camera flashes he generated was otherworldly, as if he was from another planet.

"So for our gala, what if the masquerade theme was Old Hollywood? The guests could dress up like Clark Gable and Judy Garland and so on."

After he took in the idea, Zander nodded emphatically. "I love it! And with a lot of current Hollywood stars coming to the gala and here for the film festival, they'll do it up big."

"That's what I was thinking."

"We could screen some of the classic movies in areas of the party space, as decor."

"You said you wanted to do a custom cocktail. Maybe that could relate to the theme?"

"Fantastic. I think you've solved how we're going to create the most memorable event of the season. Let's make some notes. Can I get you a brandy, or some tea?"

"Tea would be nice. You've got your hands full with the baby. I can get it for us if you'd like."

Heartened by the coziness of her offer coupled with the unfamiliarity of a woman used to fetching her own drink, he lifted a free finger to point. "Help yourself to anything in the kitchen."

Returning with a couple of mugs, she set them down on the coffee table. "I would love to get out of this dress and heels, so I'll take Iris up on her offer if you'll excuse me."

While she was gone, Zander managed to toe one shoe off and then the other without disturbing the baby.

The sight of the two mugs, with the tea bags still seeping in the hot water, touched him with their domesticity.

His jaw twitched when Marie came back into the room. In yoga pants and a plain T-shirt, she was as pretty as she'd been in the lavish gown. Barefoot, she zhooshed her hair until it looked like the slightly messy style she usually wore.

"What are you staring at?"

He hadn't realized that his gape was so blatant.

The sharp contrast to the glitz of the Carlsmon struck him like a lightning bolt. This was what life was. Yoga pants and tea bags and needy babies. It was what he was only first learning about, how to be a parent. Lessons that would take him a lifetime. Some that he would never learn.

He'd never before visualized the passage of years now running across his mind like a timeline. Abella gaining new skills as she prepares to start school. Then the schoolgirl years in the stiff uniforms. Which would be followed by the teenage years with battles for independence. She might be brought up as a royal and go to all the best schools but Zander was determined that she'd experience some of the same phases any other child would.

It occurred to him what it might be like to go through all of that with someone. A partner. To raise a child together. The right some-one, of course, not some phony like Henriette or the women his mother fixed him up with.

Maybe to have children of his own some-day. Effectively giving Abella a sibling or two.

With him and Elise raised by palace staff as their mother was too busy jet-setting around the world to be bothered, every day he un-derstood more and more about why his sis-ter was adamant that Zander be in charge of Abella were anything to happen to her and Valentin. To not let Claudine hold the reins.

Parenting was serious business. It had begun to worry Zander that although he might develop into a reasonably worthy fa-ther, Abella would need a mother figure in her life, as well. If not even more importantly than she'd need him.

He wondered about life in a typical fam-ily's home. Laughter and tears, triumphs and defeats, shared together as a team. To be loved as a man, not a prince. With a woman who brings him a cup of tea, and just as often he brings one to her. Was that what he was coming to long for?

And why, of all people, was it Marie who lit that yearning in him?

It dawned on him that for all the years he'd

spent globetrotting with his significance and position opening any door he wanted, he'd been doing his mother's bidding. She wanted him married properly and orchestrated a lifestyle that would put him on that journey as soon as he reached adulthood.

Yet in all that time he'd never met anyone who touched him inside the way Marie did. With those opaque blue eyes of hers that seemed to go from compassionate to wounded to intelligent and then back again. What made her tick? Somehow, more than anything, he wanted to know.

To her question of why he was staring he offered only, "Sorry. Please make yourself at home."

Which she did by sitting on one of the sofas and tucking her legs under her. Again, the informality of her position plucked at heartstrings he never knew he had. He sat down next to her, the baby stirring a little bit to sprawl herself farther across his chest.

"Babies are perfect, aren't they?" Marie tilted her head to watch Abella's face as she slept.

"They don't know enough not to be."

Was Marie aware of how perfect *she* was? Zander sensed she didn't, that the hardships she'd known had damaged her self-esteem.

"I'm sure what's going through Abella's little brain is that she's safe and cared for in your arms."

"Do you think about having children?"

"I'm afraid I wouldn't know how to do it. I didn't have the best examples of motherhood in my life." Funny enough, neither had Zander. "It looks like you're doing a great job with Abella so far."

Golden light shone through him at that.

"That's the greatest compliment I could ever receive."

"I respect how seriously you take your obligation toward her. Not every relative of an orphan does."

"You'd said that no relatives took you in after your parents died. What did happen?"

"Honestly, right afterward I was in kind of a daze."

"You were just eleven."

"I was put in someone's home temporarily. I think it was for about a week. They barely spoke to me. I was terrified. They didn't really have room for me and I remember sleeping on sofa cushions on the floor without a blanket. It was very cold."

Zander swallowed hard at that disturbing retelling.

Marie clenched and then released her fists.

He pointed to her hands. "I notice you often doing that."

"Nervous habit I suppose." She reached for her tea and wrapped both hands around the warm mug. Her eyes downcast.

He kissed the top of Abella's head, the baby sound asleep in his arms. "Then you were placed in longer-term foster homes? Were you treated lovingly?"

Marie shook her head no without making eye contact. "In none of them."

"And by your parents?" She signaled no again.

"Look at what you've done for yourself, Marie. After all of that, you made it through university and you have a career. You're amazing."

She smiled.

"Let me put Abella in her crib."

When Zander returned, he sat down close to Marie. Her expressive blue eyes were clouded from the late hour and perhaps the conversation. The plump lips that no longer held the red lipstick of the evening looked clean and...

Kissable. Irresistibly kissable, he thought as he leaned toward her. And unlike the peck on the cheek or the arm around her shoulder that had come before, what happened next was not spontaneous. It was not accidental.

No, as Zander brought his mouth to Marie's, the kiss he gave her had to have communicated that it was deliberate. The dominance with which he took her lips, kissing her once, then twice, then longer, bounded from inside him and wouldn't be denied.

"Marie." He suddenly pulled back. "I'm so sorry. The hour is late and…"

She looked to him with those big glassy eyes, half-shocked but clearly aroused, whispering, "Don't stop."

And he didn't. What his heart and body told him superseded any mental wisdom. He could experience her only with all his senses.

The peeking of her collarbone above the neckline of the T-shirt. The fragrance of her warm slinky skin. The taste in her mouth, like the juiciest fruit of summer. The tiny sigh that escaped from her lips. The strands of shiny hair through his fingers as he pulled her in for more electrifying kisses that he'd remember for the rest of his life.

After the last good-night kiss at the door when his driver arrived, Zander had dropped down onto the sofa, where he lay for hours, drunk on Marie.

Sometime during the wee hours, he concluded that it would now be impossible to deny that things had changed between them. Tonight's kisses were not at all like the physical contact they'd had before, which could maybe be construed as platonic affection. What was rocking through him was a truth that wouldn't be fooled.

Yes, he'd have to tuck it right back inside. He wasn't in a position to let anything develop between them. It was unfair to risk that she might feel otherwise. He really didn't know how she'd regard tonight's kisses. If she understood them as he had. An acknowledgment of their magnetism toward each other, but as an isolated incident. The last thing he'd want to do is hurt her.

The kisses had gone too far. A surge of carnal male desire combined with the camaraderie that had grown between them prompted him. The voluptuousness of her lips received many of his tender kisses. Which was then followed by a long one that was different, a penetrating kiss that lasted for five minutes and inhabited his entire body, making him lunge to her for more.

All told, Zander hadn't been able to contain himself until he'd kissed Marie probably twenty times. And was barely able to maintain the gentlemanly decorum he'd prided himself on, and the paternal concerns that now informed every move he made. In fact, he'd come quite close to letting go of all restraint entirely, which was why he'd separated from her long enough to text for his driver.

With the hungry animal in him uncaged, he envisioned leading Marie into his opulent bedroom and laying her down on the designer sheets and plush blankets afforded him. Where they'd then engage in passion taken to untold erotic heights. He wouldn't rest until he'd slowly explored all of her creamy flesh and satisfied every single longing both he and she had. And let her know that she was valued and lovable and…well, magnificent.

Unbridled lovemaking most definitely could not be on the agenda with Marie.

But a man could dream, couldn't he?

CHAPTER SEVEN

"HERE'S THE SET list from the band for the dancing portion of the evening," Zander said over bites of the salads and sips of the lemonade he'd had delivered to Marie's office.

The week had been a whirlwind. With the APCF gala quickly approaching, Marie and Zander had spent countless hours on every facet of the event. Having decided on Marie's idea of an Old Hollywood theme, they looked to apply it to every component of the party. "I told them we wanted all classic songs from movies. There are so many greats here. Do you know this one? 'Love Is a Many Splend—'?"

Marie finished her crunchy bite. Zander could have been reading from the telephone directory for the amount she was able to listen at the moment. Although she'd held herself professionally all morning, the discussion of dancing was impeding her ability to stay attentive.

All her mind could do was wander back to the night of the Carlsmon party. To Zander, resplendent in his slim-cut navy blue tuxedo. Which happened to complement her pewter-colored gown to a T.

With his big arm firmly around her waist, he'd held her close as they danced to modern ballads. In sync, like together they could dance away all the troubles in the world. Making Marie feel that, just for a moment, her past and his present didn't matter an iota. That they looked like a couple in love, gliding and laughing as if they were totally alone rather than in a crowded ballroom filled with the wealthiest and most beautiful people on earth.

Remember, she told herself now in the confines of her spartan office, Zander was one of those people. She was not. Although she'd told him a bit about her traumatic adolescence, he didn't know even the half of how different they were, and she hoped he never would.

"'… Are a Girl's Best Friend,'" Zander finished the set list she hadn't been listening to, so fixed was she on the tones in his voice.

As much as she'd tried to forget the kiss on the cheek and his arm around her shoulder at the Mexico benefit, those were nothing com-

pared with the kisses at his apartment after
the Carlsmon party. Because, with a reason-
able amount of feasibility, the peck and the
arm around her shoulder might have been
chaste exchanges between colleagues. Although, really, even those encounters were
tinged with flirtation and romance, unless
she had imagined it.

But at his apartment? No way were those
kisses between coworkers, or even friends.
As she watched Zander bring his lemonade
to those sumptuous wide lips, her body shud-
dered at the recollection of his mouth on hers.
Those lips that, with the smallest of movements, had taken her on a wild ride of yen
rewarded with pleasure.

At the stem cell research fund-raising yacht
party last night, they'd moved together as a
choreographed unit. She'd worn the blue gown
with the beaded overlay, and Zander wore his
tuxedo with a blue shirt that almost matched
the hue. There was no division between where
one of them ended and the other began. As
they finished each other's sentences with a
jovial banter that seemed to charm the scien-
tist crowd on the boat that night, Marie had
become more and more comfortable with the
schmoozing and increasingly optimistic that
their own gala would be a success.

Simply put, they worked well together. That was when she loved her job the most. Collaboration, when everybody was looking in the same direction, focused on one outcome, the success of the event. It was almost as if those involved became a family for the duration. It was a feeling that gave her immense satisfaction.

But she needed to watch herself around Zander. He already had a family, the royals on Charlegin and what he was creating with Abella.

There was no question in her mind, though, that she'd never been attracted to a man like she was to Zander. She was a moth to his candlelit flame. That night after the Carlsmon party and, if she was being honest, since the moment she met him she had been drawn to him.

To his sincerity. To the way he wielded his power with a quiet control. To his compassion. How he made her feel connected to him. And the way he was with Abella. Watching him so careful, so attentive, so decisive about what she needed was one of the most heartwarming displays Marie had ever witnessed. It wasn't just flattery when she told him how good a job she thought he was doing with her.

Nothing would ever come between him and

his care for Abella. Rather than wishing it was otherwise, Marie was grateful to know that Abella was going to receive a lifetime of loyalty and support and love even without parents. What she'd never had. A woman would be wrong to try to pull Zander from Abella's plight. Marie was happy for the baby princess.

So she'd forever treasure those life-affirming kisses from Zander, and expect nothing more. Neither one of them had instigated talking about those kisses. That Zander hadn't brought them up reinforced to Marie that they weren't important to him. Which kept her from mentioning them.

"I've got to get home." Zander finally declared after a productive afternoon. They stood. He packed his computer bag, gave Marie a very European kiss-kiss on both of her cheeks and then headed out her office door.

His departure brought a lurch forward to her shoulders as she watched the back of him stride down the corridor. Of course, she wanted him to leave and get home to the baby, who would probably be as delighted to see him as Marie was sad to have him go. Nonetheless, she'd count the minutes until she saw him again tomorrow.

Rage tasted bitter in her throat as she recalled the facts about her parents that she'd never tell Zander. Tamma and Bruno Paquet headed a ring of drug dealers that supplied illegal methamphetamines to the already downtrodden residents of the council blocks where they lived. When Tamma and Bruno discovered that their inventory had been stolen, they took to the street to confront the rival drug gang that also staked claim in the neighborhood. Whose members proceeded to shoot Marie's parents to death in the middle of the afternoon.

Unknowing and unprotected eleven-year-old Marie was in their shoddy apartment while it happened, even hearing the gunshots coming from the street, although she didn't know it was the sound of her becoming an orphan.

As Zander's broad shoulders, long legs and golden hair turned the corner and she couldn't watch him walk away any longer, unwelcome tears welled behind Marie's eyes. As she had been taught to in counseling, she concentrated on labeling her feelings.

Anger again. That was what it was. She was bona fide furious that she'd met very few men in her life whom she would consider of high quality. The kind of men who were secure in themselves. Who treated everyone with respect. Men who thought it worthwhile to see that others around them felt safe. Who communicated clearly when they were speaking and who genuinely listened.

Zander was that kind of man.

The kind she'd never have.

The only men she ever attracted were insecure types like Gerard, who found some kind of sport in pointing out their superiority. Or the few other damaged men she'd dated who weren't responsible, and she'd become their surrogate mother and caretaker.

She had never witnessed a healthy relationship in action. Her parents were two irrational people, in her memory, always dressed in ill-fitting tracksuits, yelling at and accusing each other all the time.

Even though she was too young to understand it at the time, she knew that her household hadn't been normal. That they hadn't been a happy family born from a couple's love. Through her odyssey of foster homes, Marie had never gotten close enough to any of the adults to analyze whether they were in solid relationships. There was only strife and chaos.

She'd learned to go it alone. It was the easiest and most prudent decision, and one she'd thought she was at peace with.

Until she met Zander.

In him, she'd seen how a real man treated a woman, a baby, a nanny, a party guest, a coworker. The person he was showed Marie a possibility she hadn't even considered.

And at the thought of what she'd never have, her blood ran hot.

She stood breathing slowly in her office doorway long after Zander had turned the corner out of her sight.

Felice came toward her and asked for an update. After Marie filled her in about the various aspects of the gala, she didn't want the meeting to end. Although she didn't know Felice well, as executive director for the agency Felice herself had come in contact with hundreds of orphans. And, truth be told, Marie wanted someone to talk to.

"Felice, what do you think happens to most orphaned children in foster care when they grow up?"

"I don't think we can make any generalizations. And we can only collect data on those whose whereabouts we know."

Marie nodded.

"But just like within any population," Felice continued, "there appears to be a spectrum. Many foster parents are wonderful and go to great lengths to help those in their care process the challenges a parentless child will have."

None of the foster parents Marie had fit into that category.

"As far as children in homes with not-as-attentive foster parents, we see some whose past has simply destroyed them and they never become integrated in society. There's a lot of homelessness. Then you have the people whose lack of parenting produces insecurities that they constantly stumble on. They may lead outwardly manageable lives but are never stable internally."

Marie shivered at the description of what could be her if she let it.

"Then there are those who are galvanized by what they didn't have growing up and are determined to have it as adults. Whether it's through rehabilitation or simply sheer will, many become successful adults with personal achievements and significant relationships. They partner. Have children of their own and create loving homes."

Which would Marie be?

After a meeting with Chef Jean Luc the next day, Zander informed Marie, "I'm flying home to Charlegin tomorrow. We have some Hungarian dignitaries visiting and I'm expected at the palace to make an appearance."

Disappointment flashed quickly across Marie's face at that news. He didn't think he misread it. Suddenly, he felt guilty that he hadn't mentioned the trip to her before this. But his assistant for the APCF gala hardly needed to be privy to everything Prince Zander had on his calendar.

Although Marie had become more than that and he knew it, despite his mental denials. And not just with regard to the kiss that had sent his manhood prowling, naked and primal toward her. No, there was something much larger going on with his feelings toward Marie. Which was why it bothered him that even a slight wave of unhappiness, one she quickly disguised, had flowed across her beautiful face.

"Are you taking the baby?"

"No. I'll only be gone for one night. After the reception and whoever my mother has invited for dinner, I'll fly back the next day." Mentally reviewing how much work he and Marie still had to accomplish with not much time left, he suggested, "Why don't you come with me?"

"To the palace?"

"Yes. I can't include you in the meeting with the Hungarians, of course, but the gardens are nice this time of year. You and I could work on the plane rides both ways."

It was a crazy idea but not without merit. If his mother happened to have invited any of the silly girls she always wanted him to meet, Marie would help squelch that attempt. And even though he knew he must not pursue anything further romantically with Marie, he liked having her around.

"All right," she answered without spending too much time thinking about it.

The next morning, Zander's driver shuttled him and Marie to the airport, where they boarded the small private plane hired to whisk them to Charlegin. After takeoff, an attendant served coffee and a light breakfast for the short flight.

Sitting side by side in ample tan leather seats, they watched through the windows as Cannes became smaller and farther away when they soared into the blue skies and cotton-white clouds.

"What are your parents like?" It was perhaps an inappropriate question to ask a prince whose father sat on the throne, but Zander didn't mind.

"My parents are very different from each

other. My father showed me what it is to be a prince. The grace of benevolent work. He taught me to treat all people equally. To be compassionate."

"He sounds wonderful."

"He is. My mother has different concerns."

Such as flying all over the globe with her friends in the fashion industry. And measuring people by how much money they make or who their grandfather was.

Looking out the plane window, he reflected on his upbringing. His father's love for his wife sometimes clouded his ability to disagree with her. Prince Hugh had a quiet strength away from Claudine, which was when Zander and Elise got to know the best of him. Certainly they loved their mother, but it was no secret that she married their father for his title.

It was crystal clear to Zander why Elise made sure Abella would be raised by him. The weight of that responsibility tightened his jaw as he watched the plane's descent into Charlegin. Abella would rule from the palace one day, and it was his job to make sure she was fit for it. That was surely the most challenging thing he would ever do in his life. He wasn't sure if he could do it alone.

"Is everything all right?" Marie asked

in the gentlest of melodies. Was something transparent in his face? And why had he begun to factor this woman beside him as part of any equation?

"I miss my sister." He felt his eyebrows furrow. "We were very close growing up."

By the time Charlegin came into clear view, Zander's mind was a jumble of memories and possibilities. He pointed to the gray stone compound and its small tower now visible through the airplane window. "There's the palace."

As soon as Zander and Marie stepped into the entrance hall of the palace, Her Highness Princess Claudine appeared from a corridor. With her hair pulled back and in an olive-colored suit with a white blouse and heels, she looked stately rather than her usual designer-label style. A nod to the visit from the Hungarians.

"Zander," she called with arms outstretched. "Where is my marvelous grandchild?"

Since his mother rarely asked about Abella, he didn't think the theatrical fanfare was necessary. Referring to the woman entering the hall beside Zander, Claudine questioned, "Where's Iris? Have you gotten a new nanny?"

"No, Mother. I left the baby in Cannes with Iris as I'm only here overnight."

"Right. No sense in all of the packing up needed to travel with her." Claudine fixed her eyes on Marie. "But you've brought someone?"

"Princess Claudine, I'd like you to meet Marie Paquet, who works with me at the APCF. She's running the gala for us."

Marie seemed unclear how to react to the introduction so bent her knees in an awkward curtsy. Zander so rarely brought anyone to the palace, he'd forgotten to brief her on protocol.

"Oh. I see. What did you say your family name is?"

"Paquet," Marie ticked out as if it was confidential. This was the same inquest Claudine had given Zander on the phone when he mentioned that Marie would be his date for some of the balls this season. His mother's obsession with social status and rank was ever-present.

"Is your family from the Riviera?"

"We're… I'm from North Marseilles."

"North Marseilles? Oh." Claudine's voice was high and clipped.

Zander could sense how uncomfortable Marie was with his mother's interrogation.

Her fists opened and closed. Marie's reluctance to say much about her past gave him the indication that she might have endured pain, fear, loneliness and even mistreatment. Which tore at his heart. She had every right to keep her past private if she wanted to.

"Mother, I trust you'll be of help to Marie with the APCF gala by bringing along some of your more influential friends. Has your Monte Carlo crowd sent their RSVP yet?"

Her Highness stared at Marie as if she was looking right through her. "Zander, I don't know that any additional guests should sit in on the meeting with our Hungarian visitors today."

"Of course not," he quickly interjected. "I promised Marie she could stroll the gardens."

"Well, then. I'll join you in the green room in half an hour, Zander."

Once his mother took her leave, Zander showed Marie to the palace gardens. The late spring had brought everything into bloom and the grounds were a kaleidoscope of color and scent. With the central expanse of grass, Zander could imagine Abella running around to her heart's content. The last time he'd brought her here, she hadn't yet learned to walk. It was still hard to fathom that one day she would sit on the throne.

"This is enchanting," Marie said after surveying the vista.

"I apologize. My mother is rather…inquisitive."

"As well she should be, Zander. You're fortunate to have a mother who takes an interest in who you spend your time with."

There was Marie, taking the high road again. Even if it caused her distress.

"Yes, and she's preoccupied with my dating life."

"So she immediately assumed…"

"Exactly."

They stared down each other, both knowing that while they weren't a couple, though recent events pointed otherwise.

Perhaps it was too impulsive a decision to have brought Marie to the palace. Did he really expect any less of his mother than a full-scale examination of any woman he'd bring home? In his enthusiasm to show Marie where he grew up and where Abella would rule, he abandoned the caution that might have convinced him it was a bad idea.

Still in the shirt and slacks he'd worn for the flight, he needed to change into a suit and tie for the official introductions. The Hungarian group wanted to discuss a trade partnership with Charlegin. Any second guesses about bringing Marie along had to be put aside.

He swept his arm across the expanse of the garden. "You're welcome to explore at your leisure while I'm away. You'll find benches dotted here and there, so feel free to sit. I'll have an attendant bring out some refreshments."

"Thank you so much."

"And afterward, we'll get down to business."

"Okay."

But he lingered beside Marie rather than returning inside and getting ready for the meeting.

"O…kay," he slowly repeated. Yet his feet didn't move. Instead of getting dressed, he wanted to show Marie every little corner of the garden. To appreciate each bloom of a flower or leaf on a tree. To point out where he and Elise liked to play as children. And he most definitely wished he could take her to the secluded benches on the far end of the property. Where they could kiss in the sunlight without risk of anyone seeing them.

There was to be no more kissing Marie, he admonished himself! Yes, her hands on either side of his face was an exquisite sensation that he'd carry to his dying day. And yes, their mouths fit each other's as if it was destiny's will. Indeed, the mere memory of her kisses caused an ache in his rib cage that he still hadn't gotten rid of.

But no, he was not going to engage in any more romantic activity with her and that was that. As if that terse exchange with his mother wasn't enough, just being at the palace reinforced that Marie and he together was an impossibility. It was true that this was his world. One she would never be happy in.

"Okay," he repeated yet again, as much an affirmation to himself than anything else. "I'll see you in a bit, then."

"Knock 'em dead."

Marie's incongruous well-wishing brought a huge smile to Zander's face as he finally turned and headed inside. He was attending the meeting as a show of family solidarity. His role was of little importance. It was simply a meet and greet. No one would be knocking anyone dead. Still, that Marie was cheering him on was so endearing he thought his heart might burst open.

The meeting went as expected. Afterward, Prince Hugh had a ceremony to attend. Claudine and Zander exited the green room and walked together in the central corridor past the portraits of Zander's ancestors on the walls.

He vaguely remembered his father's parents, whose likenesses hung above a gold-leaf table. His grandmother, Joselin, had been the crown princess whose marriage to Prince Philip—who had not been in line for the throne of his own neighboring Balfon—had been arranged shortly after they were born. After they'd married, both the royal families and their subjects had become nervous when, year after year, the couple had failed to become pregnant with an heir. Joselin had been in her forties—unheard of at that time—when Zander's father, Hugh, was finally born, to everyone's relief.

Prince Hugh was the first in the family to marry a commoner. The story went that he fell hard for Claudine when they were both at university in the Netherlands. Claudine's family was neither notable nor wealthy, so Hugh's choice of her was controversial and a disappointment to his parents. For Claudine's family, the match was a gift from heaven, as they were immediately brought into the palace fold and well cared for the rest of their lives.

"I wasn't aware you were dating," Claudine

said tightly once she and Zander were clearly out of anyone's earshot in the corridor.

"I'm not dating Marie. Remember, I told you over the phone? We're working together on the gala and she's accompanying me to some other events around town."

"You don't look at her like a colleague does."

"Must we always have this conversation? My attention is rightly on your grandchild at the moment. This is not the time in my life for women."

"Funny how the universe sometimes has plans for us that we could never see coming. I'm guessing she's not from a prominent family?"

"Mother, she's a work partner." It was maddening that his mother was so easily able to figure out that there was, in fact, a little more to the story of him and Marie than the APCF. Though he fibbed, "Nothing more."

"Then I take it you'll want her ensconced in guest quarters tonight and not in your room with you?"

"Mother!"

"Be careful, Zander. The press will have a field day with her," she cautioned and turned toward her office while Zander headed back to the garden.

* * *

There were eight at the dining table that night.
Zander, Marie, Prince Hugh, Princess Claudine, an English duke and his three teenaged
sons who had stopped in to pay their respects
en route to Russia.

Not one, not two, but three young men
with gummy smiles and frizzy hair sat opposite Zander and Marie. Claudine regaled
them with travel stories. About the time an
African statesman invited her to learn a
weaving technique unique to his native vil-
lage. Claudine asked, "Have you been to Africa, Marie?"

And about the dashing Argentine race-
horse jockey who took her on a wild gallop
through the Pampas. At each story, the three
sons guffawed with a hiccup-like rhythm that
Zander's leg under the table beside Marie's
proceeded to mimic. It seemed to be about
five sequences of four giggles each until they
subsided and left the remaining air in the dining room to go still.

"Have you been to Argentina, Marie?"

Her Highness was making a show of pointing out that Marie wasn't in their social circle,
as if it wasn't obvious. Zander had told her
that the princess herself was a commoner, so
Marie was surprised how much she'd gone

out of her way to humiliate one of her own kind. If it weren't for Zander's reassuring hand-holding under the dinner table, Marie might not have been able to contain her embarrassment.

After the Duke and his sons had departed, Marie chatted pleasantly with Prince Hugh, an affable man who perhaps had a bit too much wine at dinner. When Zander entered the conversation, Marie explained, "I think we've decided that His Serene Highness will attend our Old Hollywood gala dressed as John Wayne."

"My son will remember that I used to be a decent horseman in my day."

Prince Zander nodded.

"We'll get you a cowboy costume with a big hat," Marie added.

Claudine joined the group and started up again, "Marie, did I see you at 'Fashion Has Passion' at the Atelier Dubois benefit last month?"

"No, Your Highness. Was that in Cannes?"

"That's right, you mentioned you weren't from the area. But you were in Venice for the 'Circus for Change' ball, weren't you?"

"I wasn't."

"Good heavens, Claudine, no one gives

a bother as to what galas Marie attended," Prince Hugh interjected.

But His Serene Highness was wrong. There were millions of people in the world who did care.

In the morning after the night spent in separate bedrooms, Zander gave Marie a tour of the palace, pointing out the works of art and gifts from foreign nations that he particularly liked. They then boarded the small plane heading back to Cannes.

As he looked out the window, he reflected on his mother's abysmal behavior. Had he known Her Highness was going to act like a dog incessantly barking to scare another one off, he wouldn't have subjected Marie to it.

Zander swiped through his tablet during the flight and scrunched his eyebrows when he came across a photo from a film festival gossip site. It was a picture of him and Marie on the dance floor at the Carlsmon party, holding each other for a slow dance.

The expression on both of their faces took Zander aback. The way they gleamed only at each other, as if they were the only ones in the room rather than two of hundreds. Anyone who saw it would surely think they were a couple in love. The caption read: *Who is the mystery brunette royal hottie Prince Zander de Nellay has been spotted with all over Cannes?*

CHAPTER EIGHT

THE CLOCK WAS ticking, Marie thought to herself as she surveyed the grand foyer of the mansion where the APCF gala would be held the next night. That the success of the evening was going to make or break her career was probably an exaggeration of the pressure, but she felt it nonetheless. With Zander's leadership, everything appeared to be in order. As if it was forbidden for anything to go wrong. Because when His Highness Prince Zander set out to do something, it got done.

She watched him across the room talking casually to one of the party supervisors. How everyone didn't melt into a puddle when they were around him, Marie had no idea. His charm was so persuasive that she couldn't set herself free from it. Between attending the parties in Cannes, spending time together with Abella, the trip to Charlegin and preparing for the gala, Marie knew her dealings with him had gone far past what was required. Let alone the kisses and the intimacies. Yet all she longed for was more. More time with him, every day, every week, every ye...

Good heavens, she tried to focus herself. She'd have no ongoing relationship with Prince Zander. How many times did she need to remind herself of that? Their lives collided here in Cannes but, after the season, he would return to his travels or the palace or his apartment in Paris. Perhaps, if she got the APCF job permanently and if he continued to support the agency, she might see him now and then.

But that was it. If there had been any question, that awful visit to the palace when Princess Claudine made her feel so unwanted sealed the fate. His Highness Zander was not going to end up with sad little Marie. Who not only hadn't traveled the world with beautiful people but was the laughingstock at the council blocks she grew up in. Where she lived in Building A on floor numbers one, three and six and Building B on floors two, five and eight as she was shuffled from one foster home to the other.

Whatever Zander might have presumed her childhood to be, he had no idea how sordid it really was. Despite the bond they shared, Marie Paquet was plainly not a candidate to spend her life with the prince.

Once again, she'd found herself in a place where she didn't belong.

"Marie, can I get your opinion?" Zander summoned her and she crossed the foyer, sucking herself up as she always did.

"How can I help?"

"Do you like these?" He pointed to a sweets tray on a side table. "Chef Jean Luc has created these individual cakes that riff on film reels, back from when movies were shot on real celluloid. To go with our theme."

Impeccable skill and artistry showed in the little round cakes. Chef Jean Luc fashioned a wrap of chocolate around the diameter of each cake so that it had the frames and spokes of a film reel. Then, with design that gave the cakes a level of flourish that would surely be noticed by every guest, the chocolate strip of film swirled up to the top of the cake in an edible curlicue.

"They're amazing. I only have one question. With the desserts served buffet style rather than table service, I wonder if guests won't be mulling about. These are rather big to eat standing up. Could Chef make them smaller? In a two-bite size?"

"Look at you, mademoiselle. A party professional! Good thinking. I'll speak with him about it." Zander flashed his megawatt smile at her, making her knees quiver so much that she subtly grabbed hold of a nearby chair to steady herself. Not giving her a moment to recover, he beckoned her, "Let's do a walk-through."

Past the foyer of the mansion was a grand staircase leading down to the great hall, through which six French doors opened onto a huge expanse of lawn. It was the ultimate in indoor-to-outdoor space and back again. They descended the stairs to survey the lawn, where movie screens had been set up in various locations so that through a high-tech setup, old films would be projected on each of the screens all night long to add to the fund-raiser's theme.

"Did you choose all of the movies?" she asked Zander, looking up to him in the glare of high noon, knowing the space would be magical under the moon and constellations.

"I asked an archivist from the film festival for a bit of help. One screen will show silent-era comedies, another black-and-white horror movies, another brightly colored musicals, and so on."

"It will be the talk of the town."

"Of course it will, it's Cannes!"

"I meant that as a figure of speech."

"I know. I was only teasing," Zander said with a cute elbow jab to Marie's arm that launched tingles throughout her body. His every touch, every gaze and, to be sure, every kiss held so much weight over her it was almost terrifying.

Oh, why did she finally meet a man she could foresee a *future* with who could never even have a *present* with her? After all she'd been through in her life, didn't she deserve that? Providences were cruel.

"Let's go over the table charts," Zander commanded with a guiding palm on Marie's back. Her tongue flicked the roof of her mouth as they went back inside.

Easels had been set up in the great hall with seating arrangements and party flow charts. Marie and Zander stood side by side, studying the plans. Tweaking a couple of the table assignments, Zander seemed generally satisfied.

Taking Marie by the hand, he tugged her back up the mansion's grand staircase. When they reached the top, he turned them around so they could look down on the party space. "After the black-and-gold carpet outside, the guests enter here. This will be their first sight of the great hall and the lawn beyond."

Why Zander hadn't let go of her hand after they'd reached the top of the stairs, she didn't know. But she wasn't going to be the one to break away. She'd take every second of him she could get, filling the memory bank she knew she'd cherish forever. Her fingers in his were so right. His huge hand all but surrounded hers in a joining that felt like…like home, if there was such a thing.

She allowed herself that one split second of visualizing being a guest at this ball and arriving with Prince Zander, a power couple unified in philanthropy and love. They'd party and dance the night away, peering lovingly into each other's eyes until the sun began to rise. At which point they'd go home. Wherever the location was not important as long as they were together.

Once quiet and out of their formal clothes, they'd come together in an embrace that laid them down on lush bedding to appreciate each other's bodies and the perfection of their union. They'd make love in the truest sense of the phrase, each bringing the other the rapture and delight that was the destiny of their coupling, only theirs, always.

"I think it will make a very dramatic first

impression," Marie said with a dry throat as she pulled herself back. "So, guests descend the stairs…"

"And they'll be guided out to the lawn…"

"Or to the cocktail areas," Marie said as she pointed to the three social salons that extended from the great hall.

"Once most of the guests are in attendance…"

"The music starts and the tap-dancing troupe comes down the stairs doing their routine."

"That's going to be a pizzazz moment."

"The waiters will be passing out the Tinseltown Fizzes." Marie made reference to the unique cocktail Zander had commissioned for the evening.

They proceeded with their walk-through of every component, by now in such comfortable rapport with each other that they finished each other's thoughts. What had they even become? They weren't friends, they weren't lovers, but surely they were more than coworkers. Yet the closeness and the kisses hadn't changed anything. She was still not a woman he could have a future with and she needed to guard her already tattered heart before it tore apart.

Once they were done, they stood facing

each other. He lifted his eyebrows. "I think that's it."

"As long as everything goes according to plans."

"I'll see you at the penthouse tonight for our costume fittings."

With that he leaned down to give her a chaste peck on the cheek, and then pivoted toward the kitchen to talk to Chef Jean Luc.

As she had done every time before, as soon as Zander was out of sight Marie brought her hand to her cheek to feel where his lips had touched it, as if she could brand each kiss into her skin to keep it safe for all of eternity.

"Come in." Zander opened the door to let in master costumer Gabin Blanc. Zander had told Marie at their first fitting that Gabin outfitted all of Cannes for these events. The big man with red hair and chapped lips entered the penthouse. He wore a smock over his white shirt and black trousers, and a tailor's measuring tape hung from around his neck.

As usual, in his left arm Zander held Abella, who was delighted when Gabin gave her pieces of fleece fabric to play with. She put one over Zander's mouth and found that hysterically funny. The sound of her innocent laughter was infectious and had the two men chuckling as they awaited Marie, who ducked into the bedroom to change.

"Whoa!" Zander exclaimed to the baby when Marie returned. "Bell-bell, do you see Marie? Doesn't she look hot?"

Indeed, Marie as Marilyn Monroe was a sight to behold in her white dress and blond wig.

"Marilyn, may I have your autograph, please?" Gabin joined in the fun.

"Va-va-voom. What a bombshell!" Zander whistled, and Abella immediately tried to imitate his sound, although it came out baby-gurgly.

"Marilyn Monroe in her heyday was the epitome of Hollywood stardom," Gabin said. "You look fab-u-*lous*. But come here while I pin and tuck a bit."

Marie dutifully reported to Gabin, who had brought a small pedestal for her to stand on while he made alterations. Zander's eyes couldn't help but follow her as she crossed the room.

The white dress was a replica of the one Monroe famously wore in *The Seven-Year Itch*, where she stood on a New York City sidewalk over a subway grate. When the train passed underground, it created a whoosh of air that escaped through the grate, blowing

the dress upward and giving onlookers a peek
at Monroe's shapely legs. While his Marie
was far too modest to reenact anything like
that, Zander couldn't keep himself from noticing that her legs did look especially fetching extended from the milky white of the
dress.

As she passed by him, he also couldn't help
but study the sight of her bare back, which
the design of the dress left open. "She's beautiful," he sang to the baby, who seemed to
know what he meant as her eyes went to
Marie, as well.

"Booful," Abella echoed.

Gabin helped Marie onto the pedestal
and while Zander knew he was gawking, he
wasn't able to stop.

Never would he have guessed that he'd
meet a woman in Cannes who would come to
captivate him in such a short period of time.

Other than the changes necessitated by the
baby, he'd pictured his season on the Riviera much the same as the usual. The parties and the women who always seemed to
be around if there was an introduction to him
to be made. The last thing he would have expected was that he would meet someone with
whom he could be ordinary and honest and
not just a talking crown.

What might become of them if Zander hadn't been obliged to marry the *right* sort of woman? Marie was far more proper where it mattered than most of the frivolous girls he'd known. She cared about things with all her enthusiasm, was a force for good, and she didn't take anything for granted.

Also, *private* and *royalty* were two concepts that did not fit well together and he knew there were things in Marie's past that she was trying to keep to herself. If, and only for the sake of the mental game he was playing, Zander was ever to let public that he was dating someone she would be mercilessly stripped naked by the press. Not just once but for the rest of her life. Whatever Marie was hiding would be the top story of every royal-following newspaper, magazine and website that existed. He had the sense Marie did not want to be an open book, which was what would be required to be with him.

"She's really not my girlfriend," he confirmed to Abella in a barely audible declaration that Marie or Gabin wouldn't be able to hear.

"Girl fend," the baby yelled out, causing a pulse to Zander's jaw. Marie and Gabin turned toward them. Abella put a piece of the fabric Gabin had given her on top of Zander's head.

Gabin returned to finishing Marie's look. In her wig of blond curls, her face didn't resemble Monroe's but the costume was undeniable. A makeup artist would add that extra touch of movie-star panache tomorrow. Although Zander surely thought the real Marie was so pretty, she didn't need any help with that face.

She stepped down from the pedestal and excused herself to take the dress and wig off. Then returned to the room in the jeans and button-down shirt she had been wearing, looking relaxed without shoes.

"Your Highness, may I do your fitting now?"

"You can call me Zander."

"Do you want me to take the baby?" Marie asked Zander.

While he'd yet to allow her to hold Abella, it occurred to him that he no longer had any reservations. He'd leave it up to Abella and read her reaction. The baby stretched her arms toward Marie, who took her from Zander and gave a tender kiss to the top of her head. Zander paused until he was sure he was confident leaving the room for a few minutes while he changed into his costume.

Turning, he heard Marie singing to Abella, *"Frère Jacques, Frère Jacques. Dormez-vous? Dormez-vous?"* Warming his heart. Certain she'd make a fine mother someday.

Playing it to the hilt, Zander soon returned to the living room. Twirling the end of his cane in his poorly fitting suit, dark wig and bowler hat, he was unmistakably dressed as early film star Charlie Chaplin's famous alter ego, The Tramp. Walking with that toddle Chaplin made famous. Marie and Gabin grinned at each other with delight at the transformation.

"I can't wait to see him with the moustache," the costumer noted.

"Look at Uncle Zander," Marie said, hoisting the baby so that she could fully see him.

"Hi, Bell-bell."

"Da!" the baby exclaimed once she made the recognition.

As Gabin made his adjustments in a final fitting, Zander liked the sight of Maria with Abella. They looked natural together. So much so that he wanted to rush to join them, to put his arms around the two females who were what mattered to him.

It took all of his will to convince himself that the optic was as phony as the too-large shoes he had on his feet. He and Abella were his life. He still wasn't planning on making any changes to that family picture.

Marie was a nervous wreck. The guests had begun to arrive for the APCF annual fundraising gala. All of the pieces had come together and the evening was off and running with a life of its own. There was no one particular thing that Marie was worried about, only that the event would be a success. She'd opened and closed her fists so many times that her fingernails had dug scratches into her palms.

The makeup artist had come and gone, lacquering onto Marie's face every nuance of Marilyn Monroe that could be applied. The alabaster complexion, the red lips, the long false eyelashes, the heavy eyeliner and even the one signature mole on her cheek.

The wig had been set into its perfect curls that surrounded Marie's face with a sexy wave at the forehead. Shoes on. Earrings replicating the ones Monroe wore with the white dress were attached, and for that matter, pinching her ears. The look was complete.

In the small office near the mansion's kitchen that she'd commandeered as her headquarters, Marie did a final check in the mirror.

"Showtime," she said aloud to herself. As if on cue, Zander appeared as she exited the office. "Oh. Hi."

"Hello, gorgeous," he replied in a tough-guy voice that completely contradicted his head-to-toe Charlie Chaplin makeover. They both laughed. "Shall we?"

With his hand on her back, a touch that had become far too regular with all the daring clothing she'd been wearing, Zander led them toward the belly of the beast. They could hear guests reveling and the swing band that was playing on the lawn.

"Any problems?" Marie asked him.

"Only keeping this moustache on. It kept falling off with the makeup artist's usual adhesive so she used a spirit gum that's like glue."

"That will be fun trying to remove later," she joked.

"Perhaps you can help me."

Marie wasn't sure why, but her ears perked when he mentioned her helping him later. They had been together so many hours in the past weeks and perhaps she assumed that the minute the gala was over, she'd turn back into a scullery maid and never interact with the handsome prince again. Yet here he was talking about *later*.

With the baby and nanny likely to be fast asleep in the hours after the gala, Zander had booked the mansion's one hospitality suite to spend the night in so as not to disturb them. Whereas Marie was just planning to go home to her single room afterward. So she wasn't sure exactly when it was that he was talking about her help removing his moustache.

How much more time had he figured they would spend together? She surely wouldn't want to get her hopes up that he meant, for example, forever, which was what she'd come to fantasize about. Did he assume she would stay overnight here in the mansion with him?

The thought of that gave her a forbidden thrill that she worked to mask.

Zander took her hand and noticed the marks in her palm from her fingernail digs. "We've got to break you of that habit or you're going to hurt yourself." She wrinkled her nose at his timing as they rounded the corner to the great hall and he exclaimed, "Here we go."

Scarlett O'Hara and Rhett Butler were the first to say hello. The green garden party dress from *Gone with the Wind* had been re-created for Madame Fournier. The bright green leaf-patterned fabric atop the huge pouf of the white skirt was dramatic.

Monsieur Fournier, whom Zander explained owned the largest chain of pharmacies in Southern France, might have had a few years senior to Clark Gable at the time the film was made. Nonetheless, he held his own in his topcoat with a thin moustache that looked well affixed to his face.

Zander and Marie greeted the guests as if welcoming them into their own home. What would that be like, she wondered, if they were really a couple receiving guests at their Paris apartment? Regardless of the glam or wealth involved, just the mere closeness of inviting guests into their home filled Marie with a bittersweet glow.

Next, they greeted Lawrence of Arabia, who took a few minutes before recognizing the prince, his university mate. "Robin Guerin had me for supper on the tennis court every time we met," Zander told Marie as he gave his old pal a pat on the shoulder.

Waiters passed out chilled glasses of Tinseltown Fizz, the custom cocktail that contained dark grape juice to give it a gorgeous violet color.

Zander introduced Marie to the guests, emphasizing her important role at the APCF. Well versed in the programs the agency provided, Marie was able to speak articulately about how crucial the evening's proceeds would be to the organization.

As she worked the room, hobnobbing with her prince, she speculated if it was obvious to anyone that she was not of their world, but of the one they were raising funds for. In hers, there was no eco-touring in the Galapagos, like Elizabeth Taylor dressed as Cleopatra was telling her about. In Marie's life, there were no shopping excursions to New York. No hula dancing in Hawaii. No safaris in Kenya. Not even a slice of pizza in Naples.

"How's everything going?" Felice, the APCF director, came up next to her, outstanding in her costume as a crazy Bette Davis in *Whatever Happened to Baby Jane?* "This is quite an event."

"No catastrophes so far."

One thing Marie knew was that if she could, she would have Zander next to her every minute of every day. A man with both the confidence and know-how to take care of the business in front of him and to resolve any obstacle that came his way. He made everything so much better and easier.

Abella was an incredibly fortunate baby, royal or not, to have this brilliant and conscientious man looking after her. Marie hoped she would always appreciate how lucky she was.

Applying every relaxation skill she'd ever learned, and trying not to clench her fists, she progressed through the party. When the guests sat down for dinner, she helped a too-tipsy Dorothy from *The Wizard of Oz*, who was holding her ruby slippers in her hand by that point, find a quiet corner to have a cup of coffee and straighten up. Dorothy introduced herself as a real-life real estate tycoon who was going to make a substantial donation in honor of Marie's special care.

Marie herself was too nervous to sit and eat so surveyed the room as dinner was being served. Once Zander noticed that she had no interest in sitting down, he stood to join her.

"The hearts of palm were a nice first course." The retro dinner Chef Jean Luc created was based on old menus from Hollywood restaurants where the stars used to dine.

"Now they have the filet mignon with béarnaise sauce and duchess potatoes."

"Then the endive salad."

"And the dessert buffet."

"Followed by Felice's speech."

"We're getting there, partner," Zander said as his hand went around Marie's waist, making her false eyelashes flutter. "I'm so proud of you."

Marie racked her brain, but she couldn't remember a time anyone had ever said those words to her before.

CHAPTER NINE

IN THE FINALLY empty great hall, Marie collapsed into a chair at one of the dining tables. Now in the wee hours and no more guests to impress with perfect decorum, she let her body languish, legs outstretched and her arms dangling like a rag doll. Staring up at the ceiling, which had been decorated with a moon-and-stars motif that made it seem as if the room was outdoors, she whooshed out a loud exhale.

"My sentiments exactly," Zander's voice responded. Marie craned her head to see him coming down the grand staircase, a sight for sore eyes if there ever was one. He'd half removed his Charlie Chaplin costume. Gone was the derby hat and dark wig. The moustache remained. With his natural blond hair, the contrast was comical.

Also gone were the oversize shoes and shabby topcoat he'd donned for the evening.

In his remaining white shirt and black pants, along with the expensive-looking loafers he'd slipped on, he took a seat beside her and mimicked her spread-out pose on the dining chair.

"You did it," he rasped.

"We did it, Zander. There's no reason to pretend I could have done any of this without your guidance."

"My princely fairy-tale powers give me an advantage."

"No. It's because of your generosity and dedication and compassion. You don't get those traits for free just because you're a royal." He smiled. "I've learned so much through this experience, Zander."

Indeed, success at an event of this magnitude was no small feat.

"You're a good student."

"Yeah, well, let's see how well I do when I have to orchestrate one of these on my own."

"Everything worked out, didn't it?"

"I think you missed the part when Maria Von Trapp in full nun regalia tripped and fell into a pan of cherries jubilee."

They burst into laughter that echoed in the din of the cavernous hall.

"What? Where was I at the time?"

"I think I saw you out on the lawn with Humphrey Bogart. Some of the wait staff came to my rescue. But poor Sister Maria had red syrup in every fold of her habit."

"Was she intoxicated?"

"To the nines, *dahling*." Marie used a larger-than-life accent.

"That was Hyacinth Jones, an American widow who lives in Sweden. She's the unofficial cougar at all of these parties, her eyes on the younger men."

"As a matter of fact, the Good Sister squealed when a hunky waiter had to carry her away because she had cherries in her shoes. Fortunately, not a lot of guests had to witness the debacle."

"I hope she writes a fat check for the evening."

Marie sat up to take off the high-heeled white sandals that had been part of her Marilyn Monroe ensemble. She crossed one leg over the other knee so that she could rub her foot. "I danced so long with Frankenstein I thought my feet were going to fall off. Then Groucho Marx wanted a turn."

"Here." Zander turned his chair and took Marie's legs onto his lap. "Allow me."

When he wrapped his two hands around her right foot, it was as if someone had just covered her in a plush heated blanket. Her head fell backward. Even if she had wanted to object she wouldn't have been able to, his fingers were *that* therapeutic. With the skill of a masseuse, he kneaded and soothed her tired muscles, first one foot than the other.

"And you do foot massages, too?"

He batted his eyelashes in an adorable way.

How much fun this was to sit with Zander and have a recap. Actually, doing anything with Zander was fun. That was something she had never faced head-on. The inalterable fact that sharing both the good and bad times with someone made everything nicer, and might even make the intolerable tolerable. And not just with anyone but to be one of the lucky few in life who met that special person who made them feel whole, complete and part of something.

Truthfully, in the dark of lonely nights after hard days, Marie's soul did cry out for that someone she thought she'd never meet. She turned her head toward Zander and something wordless but significant passed between them.

Her legs felt the jostling when he adjusted himself in the chair.

"That feels amazing," she let slip. The words ricocheted from one side of the room to the other. "Unfortunately, I'm going to have to get those shoes back on and gather my things. It's time to go home."

"Marie, I'm sorry, I let my driver go. You know I rented the hospitality suite upstairs in the mansion for the night."

"That's okay. I'll just call a rideshare."

"At this hour? No. Why don't you stay here with me? There's plenty of room."

No, Marie. Whatever you do, say no to that offer. It had been a struggle all along to keep her attraction to Zander under wraps. She'd endured the casual touching and the not-so-innocent kissing. How much further could she go?

Oh, those kisses.

Bliss rang through her as she recounted the night of the Carlsmon party, replaying every second of what were most certainly the most exciting kisses she'd ever had. Marie's mouth yielding to Zander's. Accepting his every move. Initiating some of her own. Their lips, their tongues, fitting exactly to each other's. Both wanting more, knowing to deny themselves. Her eyelashes still flickered every time she thought of those kisses. They probably always would.

It would be too risky to share the suite with him tonight, regardless of the sleeping arrangements. That proximity would fill her head with too many what-ifs, silly unrealities about things that could never happen. Like making love. Like until eternity. The stuff dreams were made of.

"No." She eked out a sound that was sort of a half question. After a few measured breaths she tried again with, "I'd best be going."

She swung her legs off Zander's oh-so-comfortable lap and jammed her feet into her shoes. They seemed to have shrunk two sizes since she'd taken them off. Or maybe it was that her feet grew when out of the confines of the leather and in Zander's hands. When she stood up, she all but crumbled with tiredness. Having to take even one more step seemed an impossible demand.

There'd be no harm in spending the night here at the mansion with Zander, she decided.

The truth was that she wanted to make love with him. To experience the passion that they'd doled out to each other only in small amounts so far.

But she was too afraid of the hurt it would cause her afterward, when the certainty that they could never be together would be a knife to her heart.

"You must be hungry. I have a tray of cheese and fruit waiting for a bedtime snack," he coaxed as he rose from his chair.

He moved over to one of the waiter stations. From a silver ice bucket, he extracted an unopened bottle of frosty champagne. And from the glassware cart he threaded the stems of two crystal flutes in his fingers.

After a kind smile that pierced into her weary eyes, Zander lifted Marie into his arms.

A moan escaped from her throat as she wrapped her arms around his neck. Like it was the most normal thing in the world.

As they kept their gaze on each other, he carried her up the grand staircase.

Once in the suite, Zander gently placed Marie down. She immediately stepped out of her shoes, grateful to be barefoot again.

The two-room suite was as well designed and tasteful as the rest of the mansion. Built in the 1800s, it had been upgraded with every modern convenience anyone could want. The sitting room furnishings were done in dark woods and the upholstery a forest green. French doors were left open to allow in the moonlight and cool night air. To one side was a separate bedroom with a gigantic bed, carved wood posts and a dozen inviting pillows.

"May I freshen up a minute?"

"Of course," Zander replied as he uncorked the champagne bottle. He gestured toward the bathroom.

There, marble walls and surfaces were accented with gold fixtures. A glass shower had a built-in bench inside and a rain shower faucet. It looked glorious, though if Marie did use the facilities, she'd probably rather try the soaking tub. It was big enough for two people to fit in, and the whirlpool jets promised to turn sore muscles to jelly.

For now, though, she opened the taps of the sink to bring the water to a tepid temperature. Needing a bar of soap, she turned to the generous basket of toiletries that had been provided. With three options to choose from, she brought each to her nose and decided on the invigorating lemon cucumber bar. She washed her face and hands and dried them on one of the thick towels.

If she wanted to wash her hair later, she noticed that there were swanky shampoos and hair conditioners in the basket. There were lotions. Toothbrushes. Toothpaste. Deodorant. Sunscreen. How nice.

And look at that!

The basket even contained a package of condoms. She lifted the small cardboard box, tastefully white with a gold seal. If the contents were to be required, one would only have to tear the seal to open it.

How very modern and thoughtful.

Condoms.

* * *

A thousand people had populated the mansion for the gala. From the suite on the second floor, Zander could no longer hear a sound below. The staff had done as much cleaning as they'd intended to for the night. Rented tables, chairs and dinnerware would all be picked up in the morning. He knew there were security people somewhere on the premises downstairs, but they were silent.

It was just him and Marie, munching cheese in the hush of this enormous property.

"Have you ever grown a real moustache?" Marie asked Zander as they lounged on the settee in the sitting room of the suite. The Charlie Chaplin version the makeup artist had adhered to his face remained. "What does it feel like?"

"I attempted to grow one at university. It was itchy at first," Zander recalled. "It came in rather scruffy and prickly. Mother hated it. Girls I dated while I had it never said anything, so I don't know what they thought. Because, of course, one doesn't criticize a prince's choice of facial hair."

He knew he bit that out with some sarcasm. But it was absolutely true that he'd never been with a woman who had been honest with him about anything, let alone something as small a matter as his facial hair.

Except for Marie, resting beside him on the settee, never trying to be anything she wasn't.

Her pretty and sore feet were curled up between them. It had been almost unbearably personal rubbing them in the dining room before they came upstairs. Though his thumbs so enjoyed working on all of the muscles in between the delicate bones.

Was massaging someone's feet a gift of love to them? One he was unused to bestowing or receiving? In any case, having her silky legs on his lap had been unexpectedly arousing.

Zander's mother, dressed as Holly Golightly from *Breakfast at Tiffany's*, complete with long cigarette holder, had cornered him at the gala to ask again about Marie. Apparently she still wasn't convinced by the *just coworkers* label he had been insisting on.

"You know the press will rip her to shreds," Claudine had told her son, buzzing into his ear as they watched Marie being dragged around the dance floor by a lead-footed Ben Hur.

"The press doesn't know who she is, Mother." He thought of the headline he'd caught in his news feed that questioned who the *mystery woman* was whom Prince Zander had been spotted with in Cannes. "Working for the APCF is hardly high profile."

"They'll find out, I promise you," Claudine pressed.

Zander pushed those thoughts away. They weren't together, despite his mother's assumptions. Marie's life was none of anyone's business but hers. Besides, what could be in her past that was so newsworthy?

He reached to the corner of his mouth and began to peel away the fake moustache. It wasn't as easy as it seemed. The spirit gum the makeup artist had used proved quite effective. He worked on it a smidgen at a time but without much success.

"This moustache was made to last. I can't get it off."

"Do you want help?" Marie asked.

"I think I might need some."

She unfurled her curvaceous legs and turned to face him on the settee. Leaning in, she used a fingernail to pick at the outer edge.

His entire body immediately reacted to her closeness and her finger on his face. Desire coursed through him and his mind swirled with images.

Like how when he lifted her legs to his lap in order to massage her feet, he'd allowed himself a quick caress down the length of her smooth limbs.

And that now, the pad of one small fingertip on his face was bringing a gratification grossly out of proportion to the action she was performing. It didn't matter, though. He wanted to enjoy every minute.

He shut his eyes, her face so near as she studied the task at hand. Was he imagining it or could he feel her gentle breath tickling his skin? In any case, it was delightful and made him not want the moment to end.

"You're not kidding with this glue," she sniggered.

"Do you have any suggestions?"

To his surprise, she brought her lips to his and kissed him. Not once. Not twice. And by the third time, he was intoxicated by her mouth and took her head in his hands to deepen the kiss.

"Very scratchy!" She pretended shock. He eased up, not wanting her to experience anything disagreeable. In fact, the thoughts he was having were designing ways to make her feel anything but unpleasant indeed. He could sense her smile against his face when she added, "But I didn't say I wanted to stop."

So with her encouragement he kissed her face, knowing that the coarse hairs of the moustache would create a sensation on her skin that she either loved or hated. The dulcet hum that escaped her throat gave him the answer he needed.

His mouth sought the curve of her jaw. He kissed its expanse upward to behind her earlobe. Another sigh of praise from her invigorated him further. Next, his mouth traced down the side of her neck. Once his lips found their way into the exquisite crook where neck met shoulder, he thought he might have reached heaven on earth. By then she had run her fingers through his hair, holding his head to her, wanting this as much as he did.

Breaking for a moment, he leaned back. Marie was still wearing the Marilyn Monroe wig that had been her costume. He wanted to feel her own soft hair so he easily slipped the wig off her head and tossed it to the nearby table. She reached up to remove the hairnet that had bound her own locks, and her brunette waves tumbled down around her face. "Back to me," she said quietly.

"You are always you, Marie, that's what I love about you."

Once he'd uttered those words, he couldn't take them back.

He rationalized that saying he loved something about her wasn't the same as saying that he loved her.

Although he suspected that he might. In fact. Love her.

The swell in his heart whenever she was near could have been a clue. How much he'd looked forward to each and every one of their meetings as they'd worked on the gala. How many laughs they'd shared about everyday things like couples do. How beautiful she was with Abella, respecting that Zander took his responsibility toward his niece with the utmost seriousness. How she treated him as just a sincere man, not one with whom she had to wear kid gloves or be careful what she said.

Marie made him want it all, the real romance, the real family, the real union. She had defied and destroyed every barrier to love that Zander had been able to build.

After shaking out her natural hair, she amazed him when she leaned over and, with one ferocious tug, stripped the moustache off his face.

"Ouch!" He feigned injury but was actually relieved to be rid of it.

"There you are," she sang, "the real Zander."

He encircled her in his arms and kissed the top of her head.

She leaned her neck backward to meet his

face and they began another set of kisses, each one more urgent than the one before, communicating their depth of hunger for each other.

She muttered against his lips, "Yes."

Before long, Marilyn Monroe's dress and Charlie Chaplin's clothes were flung across the suite. Where they stayed until morning light replaced the pitch-dark skies.

Marie's eyelids didn't want to pop up. She had the sense she'd been drifting in and out of sleep for quite a while. It was only when her brain focused on the sound of breathing coming from beside her body did her eyes spring open wide.

It hadn't been a dream. Handsome, compassionate, spicy Prince Zander de Nellay of Charlegin was next to her in the suite's luxurious king-size bed. Their bodies were touching. They were both naked. No Charlie Chaplin moustache. No Marilyn Monroe wig. No one here to call him Your Highness.

Gingerly, she rolled over onto her side so that she could watch him sleep without waking him. With the shards of morning sunshine peeking in, Zander's skin and hair caught flecks of light in a way that made him appear almost holy, like a religious painting. Yet he wasn't a distant idol to be worshipped from afar. No, this was a vigorous man made of flesh and blood.

It wasn't hard to picture this scenario as a regular occurrence. Saying good-night to Zander as the last thing she did before going to sleep, and good-morning the first on awakening. Such ho-hum behavior between a couple, yet so meaningful.

She silently thanked him. For showing her a world she'd known nothing about. Not how to run a big gala or interact with a donor, although she'd surely be eternally grateful to him for teaching her those skills. What she was really thankful for was his kindness toward her. His belief in her abilities. His perception of her as beautiful and sexy and worthy. No one had ever made her feel that way. Inching out of the bed, still careful not to disturb his sleep, she tiptoed her way across the geometric-printed rug that covered the hardwood floors. Entering the bathroom, she fumbled for the light switch and pressed the door shut.

Evidence of what transpired last night was strewn on the countertop. That upmarket little white cardboard box of condoms that she had been so impressed with was crushed out of shape. The gold seal had been broken. The contents had been removed.

Did she look different in the bathroom mirror from how she had the night before? Disregarding the costume, of course, but traveling behind her eyes, inside her heart, into her very center, she perceived a shift.

Yes, she and Zander had made love. Which she'd done before, with a couple of other guys she'd dated. But it occurred to her now what the phrase *make love* really meant. And she realized it was something she hadn't actually known.

Never had she been with a man who insisted that she enjoy as much pleasure as he did. Unlike those previous men, who treated her as if she were an inanimate object for their use, the lovemaking she shared with Zander was not a score sheet tracking who was doing the giving and who the taking. In fact, giving and taking had blended together to become one and the same.

Together, they'd learned each other's bodies and responses, slowly and deliberately, bringing one another other up and then higher and higher and higher still until they folded into each other's arms as one.

And now that he'd taught her what physical intimacy truly was, she'd never be able to settle for less.

Creeping back into the bedroom, she slipped

on her dress and located her phone. A quick scan of messages showed there was one from Felice at the APCF. Figuring she'd better attend to that, she swiped to open it.

Didn't want you to be caught unaware, thought you should see this.

And below those words was a link to a website called *Royal Matchups*.

Dread invaded every cell in Marie's body as she tapped to the site.

The bold headline was enough to burn her stomach raw: His Hottie Highness Prince Zander's Shady Lady.

All the available air left the room and Marie's throat closed. With Zander still asleep, she gripped the wall with one hand as she read on.

We've been reporting about the mystery companion seen escorting Prince Zander de Nellay of Charlegin all over Cannes. Finally, we can confirm that the winsome mademoiselle is Marie Paquet, an employee of the Alliance for Parentless Children of France. She was assisting His Highness as he chaired the APCF's annual gala, and it seems like this pair has fun-raising in addition to fund-raising on their minds.

It's no coincidence that Marie works for the APCF as she herself was orphaned at age eleven. Readers following the news in roughneck North Marseilles might remember the double murder of a married couple there fourteen years ago. In fact, it was Marie's parents, Tamma and Bruno.

The pair were known drug suppliers to the dealers rampant in the troubled section of the city. Addicts themselves, they were shot down on the street in a hailstorm of bullets in full daylight during a turf war, while prepubescent Marie was home alone in the couple's disorderly apartment at the time.

Police found her three days later, unaware of what had happened but afraid to leave her room.

And it seems that wasn't the end of the troubles for our poor Marie…

Her palm still flat against the bedroom wall, Marie gasped. Zander rustled on the bed but didn't wake up.

So here it was. Everything she'd hoped she could keep private in her life so that she stood a chance of moving forward without being dragged down by circumstances she'd had no control over. What she'd omitted in telling Zander about herself, for fear he'd have nothing to do with her if he knew.

How naive she'd been! She'd never escape her yesterdays. They would taunt and haunt her for the rest of her life, as was their job. They would limit her options, decrease her opportunities, and could always be counted on to make her despair. Her past was an old nemesis that would shadow her until her dying day.

She read on.

The orphaned Marie, whom no other family member rushed to aid, was then set on a journey we wouldn't wish for anyone. Taken into the foster care system, she was shuffled from one from household to the next.

We shudder to think what Marie might have encountered in the six different foster homes she was sent to.

How dare the owners of this superficial website, purely for the amusement of gossip hounds with nothing better to do, investigate her background because of her association with Zander for a philanthropic project! How would they have even gathered that biography of her? She supposed that because her parents were criminals who made headlines themselves, there was no shortage of public information.

After some labored breathing to try to calm herself and identify her feelings, anger turned to humiliation. As it had so many times before.

She continued reading.

It was only after young Marie was introduced to the APCF that her fortunes improved. The agency was able to help arrange a work-study program for her to attend university. When scrappy Marie wasn't in classes, she dutifully chopped vegetables at the university's dining hall. Cheers to the APCF for also positioning her in their Toulouse office after she graduated.

Heartthrob Prince Zander has been under the radar of late, curiously not dating any of the world-class beauties he's been known to globetrot with, save for a few appearances with party girl Henriette Fontaine several months ago.

We know he's busy caring for his baby

niece after his sister's tragic death, trading bubbly for baby bottles. But it looks as if he might have reemerged, and found himself a genuine Cinderella.

Cinderella? Marie choked at the comparison. She looked over to stunning Zander asleep on the bed, his tall muscular body fully stretched out in comfort. Marie had no idea what Zander thought about her background, if he thought about it at all. Why would he? They worked together on a project for a few weeks. That was it.

Once he read this article, he'd be furious at her and at himself for letting her get so close to Abella. Protecting the crown princess was always foremost in his mind, and knowing that they had been followed and spied on would drive him mad with guilt and regret.

Marie needed to get out of the picture. Even if Zander felt otherwise, she owed it to Abella. If Marie were part of their lives, the press and public would seek to hound and embarrass Zander and the young princess every day until the end of time. They wouldn't be able to go anywhere or do anything without reference to the daughter of slain drug dealers. Abella had already lost her parents, which would inform everything about her life. The last thing she needed was Marie to present another cross to bear.

There was no other choice.

Knowing it would be for the last time, she padded over to the bed and leaned down to Zander. She gave one final kiss to that sensual mouth that had shared so much ecstasy with her. Every molecule in her lips buzzed from the contact. Half-awake, he elongated his arms and attempted to pull her to him in an embrace. Using all her strength, she backed away. She couldn't handle lying with him again where, in his arms, she might believe the impossible was possible.

Marie hoped with all her heart that he would someday find a suitable woman. Who could be a proper princess whom Claudine and his subjects would accept, and who'd be a caring mother figure for Abella. If the press approved of her, too, that would make Zander's life much easier.

She wanted the best for him. He deserved it.

Gathering up her shoes, Marie opened the bedroom door. In stepping through the threshold, she knew that she was saying goodbye to something she would never find again. Nothing would ever replicate the connection she and Zander had come to share. Nor would she want it to. It was once in a lifetime.

Goodbye, sweet Prince.

The click of the door as she shut it behind her was surely the saddest sound she'd ever heard.

CHAPTER TEN

WHEN ZANDER WOKE UP, he instinctively reached across the bed to seek the softness. The pillow he caressed was supple enough, indeed, but it was not what he was searching for. Although awakening alone had become his norm, he didn't need reminding that last night had been different. On so many levels.

Bringing the pillow to his face, he could still smell Marie's perfume. His core stirred at the memory of their union. Embracing until they'd blended into one being. Exploring one another, his hands, her hands, exciting, elevating, pleasuring. Her mouth moving from one of his shoulders to the other. His lips trailing down every vertebra of her spine. Wrapped around each other, caressing and wanting, until they joined in the most profound coupling. Their bodies fitting perfectly together as one.

"Marie?" he called out, needing her again, needing her right now.

Reality began to throb his brain like a headache. It wasn't supposed to have played out like this. He'd told himself all along not to develop romantic feelings for her. That they could never be together, therefore he would protect her feelings. And his own.

Yet once he'd lost control and kissed her that night at the Mexico party, they were, in fact, marching toward an inevitable conclusion. And then last night, the merging of their minds, bodies and, maybe especially, their souls was even more transcendental than he could have imagined.

There was no other way to describe it. He was head over heels in love with Marie. What he was going to do about that predicament, he had no idea.

"Marie!" he called out again, hoping that she was in the sitting room or bathroom. He tossed the bedding aside and rose to scan the suite.

Her Marilyn Monroe dress and heels were gone. All he spotted was the blond wig that had been part of her costume.

Confirming that she wasn't here, he retrieved his phone to check if she'd left a message for him. He only found one from his mother, which she'd marked as urgent. As he read the *Royal Matchups* website report she'd sent, feverish blood sped through his veins like they were racetracks. His head shook back and forth as if to scream *No! No!*

Fury enveloped him. At the press. At his mother. At Marie. And especially at himself. How could he have allowed this to happen?

He picked up the blond Marilyn Monroe wig. And absentmindedly ran his fingers through it like it was Marie's own strands. As if it contained Marie's DNA, and as if that would quell the firestorm raging through him.

Marie had deceived him! He'd thought they were being open and honest but she was withholding information. He'd directly asked about her parents and who they really were. No doubt assuming that he'd have to disassociate from her if he found out the answer, she kept it from him.

He sat in his disappointment and hurt, stroking the wig.

Until anger turned to agony.

Oh, what his poor Marie had been subjected to. How absolutely terrifying it must have been to have criminals for parents, with no one to protect her. For a child to have to live in the squalor and bedlam of lawlessness and drugs was almost unthinkable. And then that they were murdered with no provisions made for Marie. The pain he felt for her was unbearable.

Zander's mother had been right, of course, that the media would find a way to trace Marie. Citing newspaper articles from fourteen years ago and a follow-up piece a few years later, those evil gossip hounds had been able to expose her. To use the information to humiliate Zander's family, and Marie herself. That he had thought for even a minute there was a chance of all this unfolding otherwise was simply the wish of a naive boy in love.

The next morning, Marie woke from fitful hours of incoherent nightmares, sinister visions filled with bursts of violent colors and distorted human screams. Yesterday was a lifetime ago, when she'd quietly left the mansion where her Zander lay sleeping after their extraordinary night. First, the success of the gala had pumped them with adrenaline and giddy pride at a job well done. Then, together and alone in the still hours, their energy fixated on each other. They engaged in celestial lovemaking, the likes of which Marie didn't know existed.

Not much more than twenty-four hours ago, she'd lain on Egyptian cotton sheets in the arms of the strong and goodhearted prince who had entered her life and rocked it to the core.

He had treated her as an equal. Never prying about her past. And letting her fall in love with Abella, despite how carefully he guarded her. It was almost as if, along the way, Zander had come to trust Marie.

His trust. Which she had betrayed by not telling him herself about the horror stories, her horror stories. That had abruptly become public property. How silly of her to think that she could keep them private. Even people at the APCF didn't know every gruesome fact, although they'd heard similar tales hundreds of times.

But now, because of her association with Prince Zander de Nellay, the whole world was apparently entitled to slice her open and dissect inside. She could hardly fathom what it was to be him, to have every move he made be under the ever-present camera's eye that was always watching.

If only they could shut the world out and make their own rules about who was suitable for whom. Because when immersed in their own groove, she and Zander made beautiful music together. A tune she knew nothing would ever compare to. A melody she'd want to hear in her head for eternity.

Because not only was she in love with sweet Abella, she was in love with Zander.

So this was love, she mused a few days later in her solitary room. Like floating just a few inches above ground and no matter what you did, your feet wouldn't touch the floor. It could be an exquisite feeling of invincible vitality, one that inspired and motivated and gave forth endlessly renewable energy. But when all of that love was expended in vain, it was draining and exasperating and painful. A relentless reminder of what couldn't be.

As was the chrome clothing rack on wheels that Zander had sent over to hold the formal-wear he'd bought her. Listlessly, she touched the black lace of the ball gown she'd worn to the Mexico party.

She noted the details of the embroidered flowers and of the threadwork. Pati at the dress shop had told her it was made from guipure lace, a specific type that had an open design and raised texture. Marie wouldn't know one lace from the other if her life depended upon it, but Pati had emphasized what a unique gown it was.

Marie had never worn satin gloves before that night and the red pair was unbelievably luxurious. Bringing one to the side of her face, she brushed it against her skin just as Zander had with his lips.

She had to avert her gaze from the Marilyn Monroe dress, with too-vivid remembrances of Zander untying the neck of the halter and skimming the fabric down her body until she was naked in his hands. She had no idea what had happened to the wig that went with it.

Individual tears dropped from Marie's eyes.

"You know, you did a great job with the gala," Felice said, leaning her head into Marie's office later that day. "Zander will be in this afternoon to close out the books."

"What?" Marie all but choked on the coffee she was sipping. She knew she'd have to see Zander again sometime. He was committed to lending his name to the APCF's pursuits and that didn't end with the gala. But she'd hoped that some time would pass before she'd have to encounter him again.

She was definitely not ready to see him strut down the corridor of work cubicles toward her office, making her prickle in anticipation as he'd done dozens of times in the past few weeks.

It would take a while before she could lock into those spectacular almond-shaped eyes that were the darkest she'd ever seen. Or to notice those muscular hands that had held her so firmly in their grip. The brawny left shoulder that competently nestled baby Abella.

No, she needed some distance before being expected to face all of that again.

"Felice," Marie sputtered before the agency director moved out of earshot. "Would it be okay if I worked from home for the rest of the day? I'm not feeling well."

That wasn't exactly the truth, but a sickness she certainly had. The most excruciating, pounding, stabbing, scorching ache anyone had ever been asked to withstand. Being near him would throw salt on those already open wounds.

Felice removed her eyeglasses and let them dangle from their chain around her neck. "I gather something personal has transpired between you and Zander," she said, reading right through Marie. "Take the rest of the day off if you want. But I don't think avoiding him is the right move."

She knew that Felice was right and she'd have to learn how to live through seeing him again.

But not today.

Please, not today.

"Here's where you've been keeping my granddaughter," Princess Claudine chided her son as she burst through his apartment door, shopping bags in tow. "I have gifts."

"Hello, Mother." Zander met her arrival, Abella in his left arm as usual.

Mother and son kissed the other on each cheek and then Claudine gave a quick pat to the baby's head. "So cute."

Claudine reached into one of the bags and extracted a pink plastic baby's rattle. She shook it for Abella, who focused her eyes on it for about five seconds before turning away. Zander's mother hadn't interacted with young children in a long time, he reasoned, so she obviously didn't compute that by eighteen months of age Abella was on to more interactive toys. Still, it was a nice gesture.

"Come out to the terrace, Mother, and we'll have a drink."

When Her Highness called Zander yesterday to tell him that she'd be in Cannes for a film festival party and would stop in to see him, he'd bridled. He was in no mood to listen to his mother's stories about the silly partygoers she kept company with and their insignificant problems.

Since the APCF gala and that obscene gossip report, Zander had been keeping to himself. He'd taken Abella in her buggy out to the seaside, which allowed him a chance to take long, contemplative walks. But he'd been returning home by nightfall, canceling engagements, staying in evening after evening. He was in a funk.

With the spongy and colorful ground covering he'd laid down on the terrace, the area had become Abella's play space as much as anything else. Which drew a curious, and probably disapproving, reaction from his mother. Nonetheless, he seated her and poured some cold drinks.

"Does she speak yet?" Claudine asked of her granddaughter.

"She has a lot of words. And is starting to string them together."

"When you were that age, we could hardly keep you quiet. We swore you had already learned to read when actually it was that you'd memorized all of the books we read aloud to you. Whereas your sister kept silent until she was almost three years old."

It was quite a surprise for Zander to hear his mother waxing nostalgic about his childhood. They both knew that his and Elise's upbringings were left mainly to nannies and palace staff, with Claudine waltzing into the nursery for overly perfumed kisses before she was off for her fabulous evenings.

Of course, any complaints on that he had

were not as dire as the tragedies of Marie's childhood. But a hands-on parent his mother surely wasn't. Now, as she'd grown older, she'd apparently reinvented a history that portrayed her in a more favorable light.

At the mention of Elise, they both paused and looked out to the seashore view the terrace provided.

"Life is unpredictable," Claudine mused.

"How right you are."

Zander's thoughts moved to the anguish that had him torn up inside. Marie. When he'd gone to the APCF to finish the accounting for the gala, she wasn't at the office. His repeated calls and texts had gone unanswered. He didn't want to show up at the APCF again to look for her, as it seemed she was making it clear she didn't want any contact with him.

He should respect that.

But what about what *he* wanted?

"I can tell you're blue, Zander. Because of Marie?"

He affirmed, but his mother didn't need to be a master detective to have figured that one out. She, too, had read the startling account of Marie's history that the media had mercilessly broadcast to the world. She added, "Frankly, that press report nauseated me."

"Me, as well."

Both mother and son knew that were he to continue to associate with Marie, it would give the media endless permission to publish demeaning and distressing personal facts about her, and grant the public and Charlegin's citizens a license to arbitrate him and his family. It would fuel an insatiable drive for stories about them, no matter where they went or what they did.

"You know I had my share of scrutiny as a commoner marrying your father."

Of course, it was many years ago when Claudine and Hugh began their courtship, before the internet and social media exploded and gave birth to constant news cycles starving for more and more content. But Zander had seen some of the unflattering newspaper clippings about the shopgirl who had caught Prince Hugh's eye. They portrayed her as an unabashed gold digger. Which she was, but it must have been hurtful to have to see her ruthlessness spelled out in print.

"You and he persevered," Zander spat with a wry twist to the corner of his mouth.

"Yes, your father loved me once."

Her words dangled in the air.

His parents had a working relationship. Fulfilling their obligations, appearing at functions and serving Charlegin's subjects. They were cordial to each other. Although Zander and his sister always knew that they weren't in love.

There were no hushed conversations or private jokes. No stolen moments of affection. No long hours spent together.

Nothing like what he felt for Marie, for example.

"Doggie." Abella lifted the wooden piece from the animal puzzle she was playing with.

"Yes, Bell-bell, that's a dog."

"Doggie bow-wow."

"Right, a dog says bow-wow."

Abella went back to her play.

"When you brought Marie to the palace, I saw how you gazed into each other's eyes like you were the only two people on earth. And at the gala, how you interacted as a couple with a bond that was palpable."

"What are you saying, Mother?"

"That I had an ulterior motive in coming to Cannes today. I wanted to talk to you in person. To tell you that I've had a change of heart."

"How so?"

"Long ago, what the press thought of me wasn't the real issue between your father and me," Claudine confessed after a sip of her drink.

"Oh?"

"I never told you about Louis." Her mouth minced a couple of times before she spoke again. "Louis was the boy I was truly in love with. His family lived a few doors down from mine in dreadful Roubaix. Louis was a car mechanic. Blue jeans and white T-shirts, all muscle and libido. You get the idea."

Having never heard about this before, Zander was spellbound.

"My father became disabled when I was a teenager. Years hunched over factory machinery left him with constant back pain and unable to work. Mother was a laundress but didn't make enough money to support the household."

Zander vaguely remembered his maternal grandparents, who died decades earlier.

"After I met your father," Claudine continued, "I was faced with a choice."

Understanding of his mother's words washed across Zander. He laid his hand over his cheek where Marie had last kissed it. He could still feel her there. He slowly confirmed, "Stay with the boy you loved or marry the prince who would take care of your family."

"I never mentioned Louis ever again. I had no reason to hurt your father, who has shown me nothing but generosity. But I will never forget." Claudine let out a prolonged sigh before she added, "I know I wasn't an attentive mother. I think I've filled my life with silly pursuits to compensate for the love I left behind."

"And you're telling me all of this now."

"Because I don't want you to make a similar mistake." She reached across the table and put her hand over Zander's. "My greatest wish is that you follow your heart."

Were he to take his mother's advice, he knew exactly where his heart would lead him. Into the arms of the woman who had changed him forever. Learning about the terrible consequences she'd had to withstand only made him respect and admire her more. She'd grown into a brave adult who was devoted, caring and considerate. Not to mention kind and alive and passionate.

Yes, his heart belonged to Marie Paquet. He was in love with her. And wanted to spend the rest of his life with her, and didn't care a hoot what the press or anyone else had to say about it.

What's more, he suspected she loved him, too.

He wondered what his sister would think of all of this. He'd bet she'd want him to find love and to create a true family for Abella to grow up in.

"Thank you, Mother." Zander maneuvered his hand from under his mother's to on top of hers, where he gave it a squeeze.

"Now," Claudine said afterward, getting off her chair and sitting down on the ground covering next to Abella, "may I please play with my granddaughter?"

Marie glanced up from her computer when she heard a rustling just outside of her office. At eye level, she didn't see anything so went back to her work. When she heard it again, she tracked a more thorough search.

No wonder she had missed it the first time. Because walking into her office was not an adult of typical height. Bending her neck downward, Marie watched Her Highness Crown Princess Abella de Nellay of Charle-gin waddle in as if she owned the place.

She sang out. *"Frère Jacques, Frère Jacques..."*

"Dormez-vous?" Marie joined her. *"Dormez-vous?"*

The interlude was followed by a massive gulp in Marie's throat as it struck her that the eighteen-month-old didn't arrive at the APCF on her own.

After acknowledging Abella's angel-like hair, Marie lifted her eyes to see the man she loved standing in her doorway.

"May I come in as well?"

Marie's eyes felt so heavy it was a struggle to keep them open. It was almost as if she didn't want to actually see Zander, so unbearable was it to know she could never have him for her own. Yet a quiet murmur told him, "Of course."

Closing the door behind him, he moved to her side of the desk, beckoning her to stand up. When she did, he hugged her right away. Her arms wrapped around him, the rigid muscles of his back pleasing to her hands. He drew her close, which sent her into a swoon she could scarcely afford. So as soon as she had the composure to, she pulled away. That was enough.

But Zander insisted she retain eye contact. "Why haven't you returned my messages?"

"You know why." She hadn't had any communication with him since creeping out of his room in the mansion the morning after the gala last week. When they had made the soul-melding, earth-shattering love that only two people who truly cared about each other could.

"No, tell me. I want to hear it in your own words."

Marie desperately needed this. In addition to the heartbreak of knowing that she and Zander couldn't be together, she was also harboring guilt about the way everything unfolded. Getting the chance to say what she hadn't would be cathartic.

"I can only sincerely apologize for not being up-front with you. I hadn't meant to keep anything a secret but I didn't think my life, my background, was of any importance as an employee for the gala. And when you asked me to attend the events around town with you, it didn't occur to me that the eyes of the world would be watching."

"That's on me. Not you," Zander said and he reached with one of his hands for hers. That warmth that always emanated from his palm flowed up her arm. "I'm the one who's responsible for my own notoriety. Frankly, I didn't think about it, either. Since I'd been shunning the limelight as much as possible, I'd forgotten how gluttonous the gossip machine can be."

"I know you have the baby to shield." She looked over at darling Abella, who was occupying herself by touching everything in

Marie's office. "And you have your own reputation to guard."

He reached for her other hand so that he could hold both. "Listen to me. That's unacceptable, the idea that associating with you would somehow sully my character. To be spending my time with a smart and beautiful woman whose inner strength and fortitude has allowed her to overcome inconceivable obstacles. I'm proud, not ashamed, to be seen with you."

"We'd be chased and dismembered at every step we'd take. You don't need that. You need…"

"You," he interrupted. "I need you. Abella does, too. She'll have a kinship with you she would never find elsewhere. When she's old enough to feel the rootlessness of not having parents, you'll be there to show her the way through the darkness. We both need you."

Marie could hardly take in the words he was saying.

"I want you to come with Abella and me to live in my Paris apartment. She's getting older and needs to stay in one place. To have a routine. Other children to play with."

Zander was asking her to move to Paris with him?

"Instead of lending my name to so many

causes and attending all these events, I'm starting my own charitable foundation. Run it with me. We'll do great and important work together."

Again Marie's head swam from everything he was telling her. His own foundation? Operating it with him? "Zander, we're too far apart. I don't know how to live in your world."

"I love you. And I always will. Everything else will sort itself out."

When she started to protest, he silenced her by pressing his lips to hers. His hands released hers so that his fingers could caress both sides of her face as he delivered many more kisses.

There was no defense for his kisses, despite her feeble attempt. "Zander, listen to reason. You and I can't be. The press and your subjects will…"

"What? What can they do? We'll know the truth of what matters. That I love you. And you love me." He leaned down to pick up Abella. "What does the nursery rhyme say? *Sticks and stones will break my bones but words will never hurt me?*"

With Abella in his left arm, he used his right to bring Marie into a three-person embrace. "We love Marie. Don't we, Bell-bell?"

"Ma," Abella confirmed. With her chubby

pink finger, she pointed to Zander and said, "Da." And then back to Marie to repeat, "Ma."

Marie and Zander grinned into each other's eyes.

And then the little family showered each other with tickle kisses until all three of them were laughing from the pits of their happy bellies.

* * * * *

If you enjoyed this story, check out these other great reads from Andrea Bolter

The Italian's Runaway Princess
Her Las Vegas Wedding
Her New York Billionaire

All available now!